Katya's story

Christine Ottaway

Lured by lies from a Romanian orphanage into a life of domestic slavery in UK, can Katya escape and find the family she has always longed for?

Chapter 1

I was so lonely. It was like a black hole inside. It wasn't as if I was alone. I wasn't. There were always people around, but they didn't help. I tried to stop crying years ago, because I was only slapped or kicked by one of the other girls who told me to shut up. At times though, lying in my bed, I felt so sad. I just couldn't help it. A deep sob welled up within me and I stuffed my face into my pillow so no one would hear.

I don't know when I came to the orphanage. I wasn't born here, but no one seems to know when I arrived or how old I was or why I was dumped there.

School made life better. Well, a little better. Girls like me are looked down on because I have no family. There are lots of us, but that didn't change anything. You have to be clever or pretty or know how to suck up to the teachers for people to be nice to you. I was none of those things. I was small for my age and have mousy coloured hair that hangs shapelessly to my shoulders. The only good thing are my blue eyes, but they do not make up for my long, pale face and tiny nose.

The women in the orphanage always used to whisper about me when they thought I couldn't hear. 'Poor Katya. So plain and ...' the lady lowered her voice, 'stupid.' I just stood there, shaking. I couldn't believe someone could be so

1

unkind. I stared at her and she looked a little embarrassed and hurried away.

I hated my life. I shared a big, draughty bedroom with seven other girls, and nothing was my own. We had a small cupboard by our bed, and we could put our possessions in there, but everyone looked at everyone else's stuff and took anything they liked. The bedding was old, the floorboards cold and bare apart from a few worn mats and the curtains hung thin and faded. They didn't keep out the light in summer or the cold in winter.

We didn't even have our own clothes. There was just a big pile of items, and you took whatever you fancied each day. Even if someone gave me a dress that was just for me, it would go to the wash and when it arrived back it would be lumped in with everything else.

I longed for my own space, my own bed, my own clothes, and my own doll. Just anything that was mine and mine alone. Rolo was all I had. I don't know where my scruffy little bear came from, but I imagined he had been left with me when I came here. All my life I clutched him but when I started school one of the ladies gently prised him from my fingers.

'I'll look after him till you come back,' she said.

I sobbed, but she was as good as her word and when I came home she handed him back to me. Every day she kept him safe, but when I was older, I found a special hiding place for my friend behind the cistern in one of the toilets and he spent every day there. At night, I grasped him under the covers and whispered my dream of being part of a family to him.

I liked reading because I could escape into the stories. After school each day, whilst everyone else sat on the floor or the lumpy sofas in front of the ancient television, I read a book. I had a special corner behind the brown sofa where I could snuggle up and disappear from my dreary world into the exciting world of my heroes and heroines.

We always went out for a little fresh air late in the afternoon to the grubby space they called the garden. We sweltered in the heat of summer kicking the bare, dusty earth and shivered in the frost and snow in winter. There were some rusting swings and a seesaw that had been donated to the home by some Americans years ago. In one corner was a pile of old beds and other rubbish that no one had bothered to get rid of. I even saw a rat scurrying past one afternoon.

It wasn't much fun outside. Occasionally, the ladies came outside to play games, but they could never think up any exciting ones for us, so we played the same old ones over and over.

I wanted to get away. All I wanted was a normal home and a mummy and daddy to love me.

Katya's Story

Chapter 2

Serena arrived like a breath of fresh air. She was pretty with dark wavy hair, big brown eyes and she was always smiling and laughing. Even here.

She took one look at me. 'Katya. You and I are going to be friends.'

I stared at her wide-eyed. *How did she know my name?*

'That would be nice,' I stammered and smiled.

'How old are you?'

'Ten. I think.'

Serena laughed at that. 'Well, I am twelve.'

She put her arm around my shoulders and asked me to show her round. Some of the other girls glowered at me. You could see them thinking why has Serena chosen little Katya. I would make a better friend. But Serena chose me. No one has ever chosen me for anything before.

I showed her our bedroom and her bed. One of the other girls had recently become 18 and so had to leave the home, making a bed free. Serena was interested in everything, even the terrible bathrooms with cracked mirrors and the toilets with no doors that we had to clean most days. She didn't even seem to mind the dreadful smell of cooked food that hung in the air.

She was being so kind that I asked the forbidden question. 'Why have you come here?'

'Oh!' She laughed in that carefree way that I came to love. 'My parents live on a smallholding out in the country. I'm the eldest, but they kept having babies. I wasn't going to be an unpaid nanny or skivvy.'

She grimaced. 'They said I must either work for my upkeep or go. They even suggested I beg in town. Not likely. I chose to go.'

'But why would anyone want to come here?'

She shrugged. 'It's warm and they give you three meals a day.'

'But the food's terrible.'

'Better than no food at all. I only had one meal a day at home. This place will do.'

I shook my head. Fancy preferring to be here than with a family. I knew where I would rather be.

It was Saturday, so we were not at school. The gong sounded for lunch, but no one rushed. We lined up for a bowl of watery soup with a few vegetables floating in it and a thick slice of dry, tasteless bread.

Serena tucked in like it was a feast. The rest of us dipped our bread into the soup to make it easier to swallow.

'We have to help with the little ones now,' I said.

Serena pulled a face. 'I was trying to get away from that.'

'You can wash up if you prefer.'

'No. I'll come with you and help. We don't have to change nappies, do we?'

She wrinkled her pretty little nose in disgust.

'I'll do yours if you like but you have to give them their bottles.'

In the nursery, I picked up one little boy who was standing in his cot rocking back and forth. He gurgled and chuckled as I bounced him up and down and snuggled him. There were about 20 wooden cots in the room, with only enough space between them for someone to get to the babies. When Serena went and held out her arms to another little girl who was standing rocking, she dropped back into the cot and started wailing.

'Here.'

I passed the little boy to Serena who held him at arm's length as he did smell rather bad. I picked up the crying baby girl and cuddled her until she was quiet.

'Katya's touch.' One of the ladies who looked after the children smiled at me. She took the little boy, who was beginning to grizzle from Serena. 'You obviously don't have it.'

Serena pulled a face at the lady's back as she took the boy away to clean him up. I showed her where to get the bottles, some of milk and others of carrot juice. Then we sat around the nursery with a few of the other girls and fed the little ones and changed them.

After their bottles, we took them into the playroom and played and sang to them even though there weren't many toys for the children to play with. This was the time the ladies who worked in the nursery had their lunch, but when they were finished the children were put back into their cots for a nap.

'I like being with the babies,' I said to Serena as we wandered outside. 'It's peaceful and they giggle if you tickle them.'

She made a face. 'Better than cleaning toilets I suppose.'

I didn't tell her that we would have to do that tomorrow.

We sat under a tree on a small patch of grass in the garden.

'Do we go to school, Katya?' Serena asked as she plucked some of the grass.

'Yes. Didn't you go before?'

'Not often. The nearest one was a few kilometres away and my parents couldn't afford it. I can read and write but I'm looking forward to going back to school.'

'The boys and girls at school are not very nice to girls like us.'

'Don't worry. I can handle them. I need to get better educated.'

'Why?'

'I have plans.'

She looked at me with raised eyebrows and grinned.

Chapter 3

Katya! Wake up!' A voice was hissing in my ear.

I prised open my eyes to see Serena shaking me.

'Come on.' She giggled.

It was the middle of the night. I rolled out of bed, not at all sure what Serena was up to. I rubbed my eyes to try and get them to open properly.

'Follow me,' she whispered.

We tiptoed out of the dormitory, along the corridor, avoiding the creaking floorboards by walking close to the wall. We sneaked down the stairs. At the bottom, we checked to make sure all was quiet and everyone was in bed. I had no idea where we were going.

Serena led me through the dining room, lit by moonlight streaming through the windows, making it easy to avoid the tables and benches. We crept into the kitchen. Serena stretched up behind a big jar of flour and dug out a key. How did she know it was there? It opened the store cupboard and laughing, Serena took a loaf of bread. She carefully locked the door again and replaced the key.

We retraced our way back to our room, but I forgot about the creaky floorboards. A loud squeak just outside the staff bedrooms sounded deafening in the stillness. We stopped and held our breaths, but no one called out or came to see what we were doing. Back in our dormitory, Serena shared out the loaf with anyone who was awake.

'You'll get into terrible trouble,' one of the other girls said.

Serena shrugged. 'No, I won't. They'll never know who took it.'

'We better clear up all the crumbs.' I used a dirty sock to sweep the floor.

Next morning, the director gave us all a telling off for stealing bread. Everyone looked surprised and innocent, some because they were and the rest because they were trying not to look guilty. The director hid the store cupboard key in a different place after that.

Serena wrinkled her nose and tossed her head. 'I'm not doing that again anyway.'

She shrugged. 'Like to keep them on their toes. Something different every time. More fun that way.'

Even when she was not being mischievous, she made me laugh. She could imitate anyone, especially the ladies who looked after us. Some of the girls loved it when she mimicked the director. Serena would stand, strike a pose, and wave her finger.

'Girls! I will not have you stealing food. Anyone caught doing so will be punished severely.'

A few of the girls laughed but most tried to tell Serena off. She ignored them.

Serena was very grown up. She loved looking at any ladies' magazines that the home had been given. She would pore over the pictures.

'That dress is amazing. Don't you think, Katya?'

I nodded.

'I'd love to get my hair styled like that,' she said pointing to a photo of a glamorous model.

'You'll never have the money,' I said.

Serena smiled at me. 'Wait and see.'

Occasionally she would even comment, 'That hairstyle would suit you, Katya. Would you like me to cut your hair?'

'No!' I backed away from her. 'Suppose it went wrong. We'd get in awful trouble.'

She fingered my straggling hair. 'Better than this.'

My bottom lip trembled.

'Don't cry. You're my friend, Katya. I love you just the way you are,' she said, giving me a hug.

Often, as she was choosing clothes from the pile in the morning, she would turn to me.

'What do you think, Katya? Shall I wear this top with these trousers or does this one go better?'

I just used to grab anything that fitted. Not Serena. She would carefully pick through the heap till she found exactly the right combination.

'There,' she said, pirouetting like a model. 'What do you think?'

'Fantastic!'

She looked amazing and much older than her age.

She may not have been to school much, but that didn't hold her back.

'Are you stuck again, Katya?' she would say as I spent ages trying to make sense of my homework. 'Here. Let me help.'

She read what I was doing.

'That's easy. Look.'

And in a moment, she had made it plain.

I liked being with Serena. Life was never dull. She was always up to something.

'I told you, Katya. I have plans.'

'But what?'

'Wait and see. I'm not staying in this place forever.' Her eyes sparkled. 'There's a world out there to see, Katya.'

Some days on our way back from school, she took me a long way round so we could look in the shops, especially the clothes shops.

'Look at those clothes. Do you think that dress would suit me?'

'Yes.' I laughed. 'If you had any money.'

'I will. One day.'

It was whilst we were on our way back home from school that we met Maria. I wish I had never seen her. She ruined all our lives.

Chapter 4

Could you help me find my ring, please? I've dropped it in the gutter somewhere.'

A woman stopped us as we returned from school. She was wearing a deep pink suit, high heels and had her hair cut in a short bob and coloured blond. Her makeup was beautiful. She looked so upset that I thought she might cry.

Serena and I wandered along the pavement edge and suddenly Serena stepped down into the road and picked up a ring.

'This it?'

A big smile lit up her face. 'O thank you so much. It was a present from my boyfriend. I'd hate to lose it.'

She dug in her bag and gave us each a sweet. I thought nothing anything of it. However, we kept bumping into the woman.

'O hello – again.' She laughed as we almost collided coming round a corner whilst wandering home. 'How was school?'

'OK,' I said and pulled a face.

17

'I'm learning English,' Serena said. She stood up straight and held out her hand. 'How do you do?' she said in English.

The lady smiled as she shook Serena's hand. 'Very well, thank you.' Her reply was also in English. 'My name is Maria.'

'My name is Serena. Her name is Katya.'

We giggled together.

Maria smoothed the skirt of her navy suit. Her lipstick was the same bright red as her matching shoes and handbag.

'I love your shoes,' Serena said.

'Funnily enough, I bought them in England. When I was visiting there recently. On business.'

'Really?' Serena's eyes sparkled. 'I'd love to go to England one day.'

The lady smiled and fished into her bag and brought out two lollipops.

'Will this do for the moment? It came from England.'

'Thank you,' we both said, taking a lolly.

We walked off down the road sucking the sweet and trying to make them last as long as possible.

Another day, Maria was getting out of her car as we passed. She stood up and waved.

'Hello. I was wondering if you would like to come and have a drink and a cake at a café I know.'

'Ooh. Yes please.' Serena sounded almost breathless.

'That'd be lovely,' I said. 'I've never been to a café before.'

'Haven't you? Be a treat for you then, won't it?'

I nodded and clapped my hands.

We walked quite a way to the café in the opposite direction to the home. Wide-eyed, I gazed around as we walked through the door. The café was quite small, but the walls were covered with pictures of Paris. Each of the four tables had a brightly coloured cloth, and we sat at a table overlooking the street.

I spent ages reading the menu before a waitress came and took our order.

'I've never chosen a cake before.' I was peering into the cabinet trying to decide which of the delicious-looking cakes I might eat. Finally, I picked one labelled 'Black Forest Gateau.' It was made of dark chocolate with fruit inside and chocolate curls on top.

Serena gazed at the cakes. 'My father took the family to a café for my birthday once. He'd been paid for some job he'd just done.' She selected a sponge thick with jam and cream.

I kept looking at my chocolate cake as I nibbled it, anxious to make it last as long as possible. Maria and Serena were chatting away, but I wasn't listening. Suddenly, they both burst out laughing. I looked up in surprise. What were they laughing about?

Later Maria walked us back to where we had met her, and we hurried back to the home.

'Where have you been?' one of the ladies asked. 'You're very late.'

'Sorry.' Serena smiled and lightly rubbed the lady's arm. 'You know how it is.'

'O, Serena. Really.'

Sometimes after school, I couldn't find Serena and had to walk home alone or with some of the other girls.

Then one day Serena took my arm and swung me round to face her. 'I've been meeting Maria. Quite a bit. I like her.'

'Do you?' Tears welled up in my eyes and started to drip down my cheeks.

She hugged me. 'Don't worry. I won't leave you.'
I looked up startled. Why would she say that? She always told me we were family. We were sisters. Now I wasn't so sure.

I hardly ever saw Maria in those days, though occasionally she would meet us both, but she and Serena always seemed to be having a private conversation. I tried to listen, but they would lower their voices. One time, Serena even turned her back on me. My lip quivered and my eyes filled with tears, but I brushed them away. Maria must have noticed.

'Katya! Are we ignoring you?' She laughed, but her eyes were hard.

Serena turned round. She linked arms. 'Sorry.'

About a month later, we were in the bathroom at the home getting ready for bed. The other girls had already left, and we were alone.

'Katya.'

'Yes.' I was washing my face, but I turned to look at Serena.

'I'm running away.'

'What?' I stared at Serena.

'I'm going to run away.'

My hand flew to my mouth, which was hanging wide open.

'Where?'

I tried to hold back the tears, but they trickled down through the soap.

'Maria has been talking to a few girls about getting a job. Having a new life in another country.'

Her eyes shone and she clasped her hands together.

'No one would ever ask me if I wanted a job and a new life.' I whispered, but Serena wasn't even listening.

'Imagine getting away from this dump. Having money of my own!'

'You're only 14. No one wants a 14-year-old.' My voice rose as I almost yelled at her.

'Well, they do for the work I'll be doing. Maria said so. She said I was very grown up looking, which you must admit I am. Maria said she will get me clothes and make up, and I'll easily pass for a 16-year-old. She's introduced me to her friend Tomas, who is setting the whole thing up.'

I know I am not very clever, but it all sounded strange. Why would a lady like Maria want an orphanage girl to go and work in another country? Surely, they could get other girls? Girls better educated and with families to support them.

'Apparently, Tomas and Maria are in business together.' Serena rattled on. 'They find jobs for all sorts of girls who want to better themselves.'

She looked in the mirror and pouted at herself. 'Like me!'

'What if you don't like it? Will you be able to get back?'

'What's not to like?' she said. 'Who wouldn't enjoy working and earning money somewhere like France or Germany or England? Who would want to come back? I don't want to come back here ever.'

'But what about me? You said we were sisters. You would look after me.'

Serena frowned and smoothed her hair. 'Well, maybe when you're a bit older, someone will ask you to come and work as well. Then we'll be together again.'

We both knew that would never happen. I rinsed my face, dried it and then ran away and jumped into bed. I hid under the covers, quietly snivelling.

Things were very strained between us after that.

Every day I asked her, 'When are you going?'

'I don't know.'

The look in her eyes told me she was lying.

We hardly ever walked home from school together. She seemed to have taken up with the other older girls from the home who were also keen to leave. I heard them giggling together about their new life abroad.

One day, Serena didn't come back from school. I knew where she had gone. Four of them disappeared. When it was dark and they still hadn't returned, the director came in.

'Does anyone know anything about these girls? Where they might have gone? Who with?' She looked at each of us in turn with her eyebrows up.

We shook our heads.

'I think I heard them whispering about running away,' one of the girls said. 'I could have been wrong.'

Suddenly, one of the others turned to me. 'Surely you know where Serena is, Katya. She was your friend.'

I looked down and said nothing. The one thing Serena nagged me about was to keep quiet about where she was going.

The next day, when they'd still not appeared, the director called in the police. They interviewed everyone, but I don't think anyone really knew what had happened - except me.

The police kept asking us the same questions again and again.

'Have any of you met any strangers on your way home from school? People who've been very nice to you? Given you things? Promised you a new life?'

Everyone looked blank and shook their heads.

'Did the girls say they were going to run away? Hmm?'

I stayed silent. In the end, they gave up. No one cared that much about girls from an orphanage.

The director called all the older girls together. 'You must not talk to any strangers on your way home from school. No matter how friendly they seem. No getting into cars. No accepting gifts. Even small ones like sweets.'

It was a bit late for that. Serena had gone and I was all alone again. I tried not to cry, but at night I found it very hard. I felt so lonely.

Chapter 5

Six months later, Maria reappeared. As always, she looked beautiful. Her hair had grown, and it fell curling to her shoulders. She was wearing a pretty blue suit and her makeup was perfect. I couldn't help noticing a very expensive-looking necklace hanging around her neck with glittering matching earrings. On her hand a ring with a sparkling stone caught the light. She came up to me as if she had only seen me yesterday.

'Hello, Katya. All alone?' She gave a little laugh and patted my arm. 'How have you been?'

I glared at her and walked on.

'You don't look very pleased to see me. Wouldn't you like a message from Serena?'

I stopped and looked at her.

'Yes. I'd love a message from Serena.'

'Tomorrow. I'll buy you an ice cream.'

'Why not now?'

'Because I want to buy you an ice cream. Tomorrow.'
Her face appeared open and friendly.

'Alright.'

I stomped off back to the home, head down and fuming. My heart was pounding. I hated Maria because of what she had done, but I was desperate for news of Serena. Was she enjoying her new life? I decided though that I would not do things Maria's way. I would show her.

The next day, I went home from school with a group of girls. I saw Maria on the other side of the road and smiled and waved. She frowned and pursed her lips and pivoted away. I wondered if I had done the right thing because I longed to hear from Serena, but Maria was not going to push me around.

For the next few days, I walked home alone, but there was no sign of Maria. I began to panic and for the entire weekend I worried and worried that I would not see her again and would never hear from Serena.

On Monday Maria reappeared.

'There you are,' she said. 'I didn't think you wanted to talk to me or get your message from Serena.'

And though her bright red lips smiled, her eyes were hard, and I knew not to upset her again.

'I didn't like that you took Serena away from me to a new life. She's my friend. More like a sister. I was left alone.'

'I know.'

Though she looked at me sympathetically, there was something false in her expression.

'Come. Have an ice cream. I'll tell you how well Serena is doing.'

I really didn't want to go with her, but she was being quite kind. No one else wanted to buy me an ice cream. We went to a different café quite a distance from the home.

'Why've we come here?' I asked. 'That other café's nice and much nearer. It's a long walk back. I might be late.'

'I like this café. I know the owner.' She smiled at the woman behind the counter. 'Don't worry. I have my car. I'll give you a lift back.'

I chose a bowl of strawberry, vanilla, and honeycomb ice cream with sprinkles on top. Every mouthful was delicious. I let the cool ice cream slip down my throat, and I sighed.

'Serena sends her love. She's thrilled with her new life.' Maria sipped her cup of coffee.

'What's she doing?' I looked up with a spoonful of ice cream halfway to my mouth.

'She's a receptionist in London.'

I gulped down the mouthful, but it didn't stop a twinge of envy.

'Why would they want a Romanian girl? There must be loads of British girls who could do the job.'

'It's for my friend Tomas. He prefers Romanian girls to work in his businesses. His friends and business associates are mostly Romanians. He likes them greeted in Romanian.'

'What does he do?'

'This and that. Imports and exports.' Maria gazed at me as if I was an irritating little fly.

I wanted Serena to be happy, but uneasiness fluttered deep inside me.

'But she is happy? Isn't she?'

'Very. She wanted you to know that it was an excellent thing that she came away with me.'

I searched Maria's face carefully as I lingered over my ice cream. Was she lying?

'I must get you home.' She stood up abruptly.

'I haven't finished my ice cream yet.'

Maria glared at me, and I dropped the spoon back in the dish.
'Couldn't you find a job for me in London?'

I don't know why I said it and I have regretted it ever since.

She looked at me and smiled in that cruel way of hers.
'You're so young and not very clever, are you?'

The blood must have drained from my face. Nausea churned in my stomach and there was a nasty taste at the back of my throat. I looked down to try and stop the tears that were forming. What a horrible thing for someone to say.

'All I've ever wanted was a family. It's not my fault if I'm not pretty or clever. No one has ever been nice to me.' I choked as tears trickled down my cheeks.

'We'll have to see what we can do. Come on. I'll take you back.'

My knees were wobbly as I stood up. Maria led me to a beautiful new car with leather seats. Despite still feeling sick,

I sunk into the car seat with a sigh. What luxury. Maria dropped me off a few streets from the orphanage.

'Don't talk to anyone about coming out with me, will you?' Maria gripped my chin in her hand so hard I was sure it would leave a bruise. 'And no mention of Serena.'

I nodded and she dropped my chin. I scrambled out of the car, and she drove off before I had hardly shut the door.

I smiled as I ran back to the home. Serena hadn't forgotten me. I hugged my secret to myself like a special treasure. But Maria's hurtful words cut me deeply.

Chapter 6

Maria's judgement of me sat like a rock in my stomach. I'm nearly 13 but I know I only look about nine. I didn't see Maria again for a few days. I sat alone in the home after school, hunched up, nursing my hurt. The other girls picked up on my misery.

'Cry baby Katya is missing Serena.'

'I'm not.'

'Yes, you are.'

'Leave her alone,' one of the older girls called Renate said. 'What's happened, Katya?'

'Someone said something very unkind to me.'

'You mustn't set such store on what people say about you. You are who you are, and you must accept that.' She put her arm round my shoulder and gave me a squeeze. 'In our situation, try really hard to be the best you can be. Moping around feeling sorry for yourself will only alienate the few friends you have.'

'I don't have any friends. Not since Serena.'

'Silly girl. Running off like that.' Renate's mouth turned down at the corners.

'But she has a wonderful new life in England.' I gasped as I realised my mistake.

'Who told you that?' Renate stared at me.

'No one. Something I heard.'

'Don't try running off yourself, Katya. It's not as marvellous as people make out. You can get into real trouble. Try making friends here and stop pining.'

I took her advice and for the next few weeks I tried very hard to join in and be friendly. It started to work. The girls let me listen to their conversations. It was mostly about the boys at school and who liked who. I pretended to be interested and laugh along with them, but most of the time I was not sure I knew what they were talking about. I was more comfortable with the younger children, but if I played with them, the older girls would not talk to me.

Once, as we were coming home from school, a man approached our group. He was handsome with a suntanned face and gelled hair swept back from his forehead. He wore a black leather jacket over a smart, white shirt and round his neck a thick gold chain glinted. His trousers had a razor-sharp crease and his black shoes shone.

'Hi girls. I'm Tomas.' He raised his eyebrows and leered, showing off a row of white teeth. 'I just wondered why a lovely group of girls like you are walking home alone? Don't you have boyfriends to walk with you?' He narrowed his eyes and raised his eyebrows.

A few of the girls giggled, but the rest grabbed hands and ran off.

'I shall have to talk to some of them and tell them what they're missing?' Tomas stood, smirking, with one foot raised on a broken-down piece of fencing.

I stood staring, knowing he was not talking about me but fascinated by the effect he was having on the other girls. They were laughing in a very unnatural way. They seemed to like his flattery.

We all walked off, but Tomas took my arm and whispered to me, 'Well, Katya? Would you like a new life too? Like Serena?'

I just stared at him. I didn't know what to say, so I nodded.

'We'll have to see what we can do then, won't we?'

I nodded again and rushed to join the others.

'What did he want?' they asked.

'O nothing.'

I was trying to look calm, but my tummy was churning. A tiny seed of hope started to grow. Maybe I would get a new life too. Maybe even a family.

The next day, Maria was waiting for us. 'O girls. Tomas sent me to ask if you would like to see his new café that he has recently opened?'

'We'd love to,' said a few of the girls, the ones who had giggled at Tomas.

'No thanks,' the rest muttered and scurried away.

I assumed I would not be invited, so I turned to walk away.

'Katya. You must come too.' Maria called out to me. I laughed as I ran to catch them up.

Together, we started the long walk to Tomas' new café. I was rather surprised to see that it was the same café that Maria had taken me to several weeks before. I didn't think it was either new or belonged to Tomas, but one look from Maria silenced me.

There were five of us altogether and Maria bought us cakes or ice creams.

'So how is school going?' Maria asked.

'Boring,' the other girls answered.

'What about the boys?'

The girls giggled. 'Costin's cute.'

'I prefer George. His eyes are amazing.'

Maria laughed along with them and asked all sorts of questions about their families and background. They answered, almost tripping over one another in their eagerness to tell Maria about themselves - loving the attention she gave them.

'You're quiet, Katya. Has the cat got your tongue?' Maria asked.

'No. I prefer to listen.'

I was fearful that if I said anything, I would look young and stupid.

After everyone had finished, Maria drove us back to the home in her new car. She dropped us off a few streets away.

'Better not to say anything about meeting me, girls.'

'OK, Maria.'

'We don't want anyone spoiling our little outing. Do we?'

'No, Maria. Thanks. Bye.'

We hurried back to the home before anyone noticed we were a bit late.

Over the next six weeks, a pattern began to develop. Several times a week, Maria met us after school and took us mostly to the café, but sometimes to her apartment. If she wasn't there one day, we all felt grumpy and cross with one another, but when we walked along the road and she was waiting, our spirits lifted. Life was changing for the better.

The first time we went to her apartment we all stood and gawped. It was spacious, with polished wooden floors and had a lovely view over our town. We perched on the edge of the large, leather sofas with plump cushions and stared at the beautiful furnishings and curtains.

At one end of the living room was a gleaming dining table with six chairs standing on a colourful rug. Two silver candlesticks stood on the table and a matching pair were set on the large sideboard along with a bowl of fruit.

The kitchen looked new and had every appliance imaginable. I wasn't sure what all of them were. I swear the bathroom had gold taps. For girls like us, it was a bit overwhelming.

'Are you very rich?' Suzie, one of the girls, asked.

We all gasped.

'You shouldn't ask that,' Nadine said, and we all nodded.

Suzie shrugged. 'I just wondered. Maybe we could be rich too one day. Own our own apartment. Have an expensive car?'

She looked at Maria who smiled, the smile that only moved her mouth.

'Who knows? If you work hard like I have. Maybe.'

'What do you do?' Suzie asked.

I looked at the floor, certain her boldness would earn a rebuke from Maria.

Maria took Suzie's chin in her hand and looked her in the eyes. 'Nosey. Aren't you?'

Suzie shivered. Maria let her go and sat down.

'Import and export with Tomas if you must know. His business is very successful. He also has bars and nightclubs in London, Paris, and Frankfurt. Mostly for Romanians and Russians who live and work abroad.'

She picked up a nail file and trimmed one of her bright red, polished nails. 'I supply his businesses.'

Suzie nodded, trying to look knowledgeable. 'Maybe I could get a job in one of Tomas's bars or nightclubs? Serving drinks? Dancing?'

She pirouetted round whilst the other girls agreed.

'We'll see,' Maria said. 'There are usually openings for enterprising girls like you who are pretty.'

I stared out the window. I was not enterprising, whatever that meant, or pretty, so I would never get a job if those were the qualifications needed.

I sighed. The hope I felt burst like a balloon and my dreams escaped with it.

Chapter 7

Y ou know I am certain I could find some work for good-looking girls like you,' Maria said one day. 'Perhaps in London or Paris. What do you think?'

'O yes.' Suzie's eyes shone.

She pirouetted around, admiring herself in Maria's long mirror.

'Fantastic. Brilliant.' Nadine and the other girls said.

'What might we do? Where would we live? Would we earn lots of money?' The girls bombarded Maria with questions.

'All in good time.' Maria went to the wardrobe and pulled out a beautiful dress. 'Come, Suzie. Try this.'

'O, Maria. Let me try something on,' Nadine said as she grabbed hold of Maria's arm.

Maria shook her hand free.

'No. Let me.' The girls all pleaded with Maria.

'You girls are demanding,' she said.

Maria slid back the mirror doors of her extensive wardrobes and pulled out a few more garments. The girls grabbed them and quickly undressed and tried the clothes on.

'Suzie. Come here,' Maria said.

Suzie pranced across the room and sat down at a dressing table. Maria opened a drawer and took out boxes and bags of makeup. She quickly applied the makeup to Suzie's face. I gasped. She looked about 18. She pouted at herself in the mirror.

The other girls took turns at being made up. Each one looked so grown up in their new clothes and makeup.

I sat quietly in the corner. No one looked my way. I couldn't understand why I was there. Tears were forming again in my eyes.

'Come along girls. Time to go home. Please put the clothes away nicely.'

'Can't we keep them?'

'What would they say at the home if you arrived with such fashionable clothes?' She glared at each of the girls. 'They'd soon stop you coming here. Do you want that?'

The girls all stared at her, wide-eyed. 'No, Maria.'

'All clothes stay here. Wipe the makeup off. Quickly.'

She handed them some tissues, and they scrubbed their faces clean.

'Home. Not a word to anyone. Including you, Katya.' Everyone turned round and gazed at me. Little Katya in the corner.

About a week later, the girls were busy trying more clothes on. They were all crowded round a mirror with makeup scattered over the counter. Maria was teaching them to apply their own.

'Let me try doing my eyes, please Maria,' Suzie said.

Maria handed her the mascara, and Suzie applied it with some skill.

'What do you think, everyone?'

The girls were too busy preening themselves to admire Suzie. Suddenly, Nadine turned and looked at me.

'Let Katya try on some clothes,' she said.

The others all laughed. Suzie even stopped gazing at herself in the mirror long enough to smirk at me.

'No. I'd rather not.'

'Go on. Try this dress.' Nadine held up a very short dress.

'I'll only look silly.'

'It'll give us a laugh anyway.' I think that's what Suzie muttered, but she spun back to the mirror.

Nadine insisted, so I put the dress on. 'Now the black tights and high heels.'

I made a mess of putting on the tights as they were so thin compared to the thick wool ones we wore every winter. I stood in the outfit and blushed bright red. Everyone laughed at me as I looked so silly.

'Leave her alone,' Maria said as I struggled out of the ridiculous clothes. 'Katya will get a different sort of job. Much more suited to her talents.'

'But what can I do?'

'There is a nice family in England looking for someone like you to help with the children and do a bit of cleaning. They're Russians just moved into the country. Business partners. Do you think you might like that?'

'O yes!' I felt quite breathless. 'To work in a family would be marvellous. Would I be a sort of au pair?' I had heard the expression at school when we did our English lessons.

'That's the idea,' Maria said, smiling in that rather unpleasant way of hers.

I ignored the smile.

As the days passed, the conversation turned from the possibility of a new life to when it would happen.

'Tomas has some new openings in his London business. He's expanding. Is anyone interested? In about a month I should think.' Maria gazed at each of us in turn.

'Definitely,' Suzie said.

The others agreed.

Nadine didn't look too sure. 'Will we be alright in England? Is it safe?'

'Yes. Just as long as you listen to Tomas and me. We'll keep you safe,' Maria said.

'Will we make English friends?' Suzie said. 'I'd like to get to know some English boys.' She giggled. 'Improve my English.'

'Better not,' Maria said. 'The English girls don't like Romanians. Especially if they think you're taking their boys. Or their jobs.'

Suzie pouted. 'I bet the boys don't mind.'

Maria stared at her. 'It's best to stick with Romanians. That way you won't cause any upsets. You don't want to get in trouble with the authorities.'

'How?'

'The police hate Romanian girls from poor backgrounds. Especially if you're creating difficulties with English people. They beat girls like you and you have to bribe them to let you go. The social workers are even worse. They'd stick you on a plane back to Romania in no time if they thought you were being troublesome.'

She breathed in loudly through her nose. 'Then you'd lose your marvellous, new job.'

Suzie huffed. 'Can't be that bad.'

Maria scowled at her. 'You do want to go, don't you?'

'Yes.'

'Do it my way or not at all.'

Suzie turned back to the mirror, red faced and cleaned her face of makeup and glowered.

Maria patted Nadine, who was nibbling her lip. 'Don't worry. Tomas and I will look after you.'

'But how will we get there?' I said, certain someone would call me stupid, but I had to know. 'Do we fly?'

'No, that would be too expensive, Katya,' Maria answered, smiling. 'We take a minibus and drive.'

'That sounds like a long journey,' Suzie said.

'It is. I'll be with you. It'll be worth it for your new life.'

A new life. I was going to get a new life. I felt all bubbly inside. Is this what it means to feel happy?

Katya's Story

Chapter 8

The day for our new life arrived sunny and warm. Excitement like a fizzy drink sparkled inside me.

I stuffed a few items in my school bag - some underwear, my toothbrush and paste, Rolo, my cuddly toy and a book to read on the long journey. It must all fit in our bag.

'Everything else will be provided,' Maria had said.

I took what I hoped would be one last look round my bedroom. The peeling paint, thin curtains, and dreary mats on the floor looked even more terrible. I was certain my new home would be much more comfortable.

Our group walked slowly to school that morning, making sure everyone else was in the school gates ahead of us. Then we turned and scuttled round the corner. Maria was waiting in her car for us.

'Hurry up girls and get in.'

Before the car door was even closed, we were off. We drove for about an hour to a petrol station on a motorway. I had never been that far from our hometown before. Once we went to a summer camp but that was in the mountains nearby. I had never seen as much of Romania as I did that day.

At the petrol station, there were two other groups of girls with a woman and a man standing by a battered minibus.

'Come along everyone. Into the minibus,' Maria said.

The girls all climbed into the back with our small bags, and Maria sat in the front. Our long journey began.

It took three days and would have been very boring if it was not for the beautiful scenery. Early on as I was gazing out of the window at the mountains wreathed in mist and admiring a rushing waterfall, the driver said, 'Come and sit here.' He patted the seat next to him.

I was happy to climb over and squeeze between him and Maria. She scowled at me.

'She needs to sit in the back with the others, Nicolas.'

'No. Let her sit here. She reminds me of my daughter.'

Maria made an irritated clicking noise.

Nicolas turned and smiled at me. 'We're passing through Hungary at the moment, and soon we will arrive in Austria. Do you like the mountains?'

'O yes. The waterfalls are beautiful.'

Maria huffed loudly. At the next stop, she went and joined the girls in the back. They were soon laughing together about their new life in England.

Nicolas told me all about the places we were passing through. After Austria and Germany, we drove into France. It was very flat and uninteresting after the beauty of the other countries. Finally, we came to the outskirts of an enormous city.

'This is Paris. See the Eiffel Tower and that big dome is Montmartre.' Nicolas pointed out the sights.

My eyes were hanging out on stalks. Nicolas pulled into another petrol station. Two other men met us, one of whom was driving a new minibus. A few of the girls went off in a car to their new life in Paris. The rest of us transferred to the new minibus with Maria.

'Can't we have a look around Paris? Now we're here?' Suzie asked Maria.

'No time for that.'

There was no more sitting in the front now and the girls in the back were very cold towards me.

A couple of hours later, we arrived at a large terminus and the minibus joined a queue. Maria handed each of us a new passport. I gazed wide-eyed at the passport that had my name and picture in it. When had that happened? I remembered that one afternoon Maria was fussing around with a camera at her apartment, taking all sorts of pictures. The other girls were posing in their new grown-up clothes, but she also had each of us sit on a chair while she took photos.

The official scanned our passports and peered at each of us and then handed them all to Maria. She held onto them as we drove forward to another booth with UK Border Agency in big letters on the top of it.

Maria turned in her seat. 'Remember you are just Romanian girls on holiday. You're looking forward to seeing the sights of London. Don't say anything to any officials unless they ask you.'

She handed our passports to the official, who inspected them and us, and asked all sorts of questions. He asked me something, but my English is not very good, and I looked blankly at him.

'He wants to know what you are looking forward to seeing in London,' Maria hissed at me in Romanian.

'Buckingham Palace and the Tower of London.' I managed.

'Maybe Katya would like to clean for the Queen,' Maria said in Romanian.

The girls all sniggered. I blushed and stared out of the window.

The officials searched through and underneath the van and a dog came and sniffed our luggage. It didn't seem to find anything. Finally, they let us go, and I breathed a sigh of relief.

'What were they looking for?' Nadine asked as Maria put the passports away in her big bag.

'Drugs,' Maria said. 'But we are not that stupid.'

What did she mean by that?

The minibus was driven into a long, grey carriage on a train. It had tiny windows, but there was nothing much to see. They packed the cars and minibus in a line down the centre of the carriage. Some people were wandering along the narrow pavement that ran alongside the vehicles.

'Can I get out? Stretch my legs?' Suzie asked.

'No,' Maria said, as the train started to move.

'Why have we put the minibus on a train? Can't we just drive to England?' I asked.

The girls scoffed. 'We're travelling under the English Channel. Didn't you know England is an island?

I blushed bright red. I didn't dare say another word.

'Welcome to England,' Maria said as our minibus drove off the train. 'And your new life!'

Chapter 9

I was fascinated. London was amazing. Red buses, black cabs, and people everywhere. There were so many shops selling such a variety of exciting things. I wondered if Bucharest was like this. I had never been there. London looked so lively, but frightening. How would I manage if I had to go shopping?

The minibus finally stopped outside a tall house in a quieter street. I couldn't wait to start my new life, but at that moment my stomach was rumbling, and I hadn't showered since we left Romania.

'When will I meet my family?' I asked Maria as we climbed out of the minibus.

She didn't look her normal smart self at all. She looked as tired and crumpled as I felt.

'O stop nagging, Katya. Soon enough.'

The other girls were taken inside, and I was surprised to see Tomas.

'Hello, lovely ladies.' His face was all smiles. 'Come along in. Welcome. You must have a shower and then a good sleep, so you don't spoil your pretty looks.'

The girls giggled and ran up the steps. I trailed along after them. I was led away from the others to a small room no bigger than a cupboard.

'You can sleep here, Katya.' Maria pointed to a small bed covered with a dirty sheet and blanket. 'The bathroom is down the corridor.'

My stomach was grumbling and my eyes gritty, but no one offered me any food. I found the bathroom, which had a shower with black mould up the walls and big cobwebs hanging from the ceiling. I didn't fancy washing there. It was far worse than the home. I climbed under the grubby blanket and slept till the next morning.

I was not sure what to do when I woke. Maria had said nothing. I tried to find my way downstairs, but all the doors were locked. I didn't want to make a fuss, but I was hungry and scared, so I started to bang on the door. Eventually Maria came looking very cross.

'Stop making all that noise, Katya.'

She gave me a piece of dry toast and a mug of strong tea. 'I will come for you later. Now, eat up and be quiet.'

It was hours later before she came back.

'I hope you've had a shower and washed your hair.'

'Yes.' I had braved the dirty bathroom. 'There was no dryer, so my hair's damp.'

Maria looked down her nose at me. 'You'll do.'

She took me downstairs to a spacious room overlooking the street. The sun streamed in the tall windows. Comfortable chairs were arranged round the fireplace and standing there were a couple who did not seem pleased to see me. He was a well-built man with dark hair, gelled down and with a bald patch glinting at the back of his head. His black eyes inspected me in an unfriendly way. She was tall and thin, her dark hair pinned back. She had a sour face and her lip curled in disgust as she stared at me.

'Here she is,' said Maria with a big smile on her face. 'Katya, say hello to Mr and Mrs Belanov. They are going to give you a new home. Aren't you lucky?'

The couple were scowling, but I tried to smile prettily and curtsied as polite Romanian girls are taught. There was no smile or acknowledgement in return.

They said something to Maria in what sounded like Russian, and she answered them in the same language. A few angry words were exchanged with everyone glaring at me.

Then Maria said to me in Romanian, 'Katya. Fetch your things. Mr and Mrs Belanov are leaving now to take you to your new home.'

My stomach churned, and I felt quite sick at the thought of going with this unpleasant couple, but I had no choice. Mrs Belanov gripped my hand as we went out the front door. Maybe they would be nicer when I met the children. More cross words were exchanged as Mr Belanov unlocked the car. Whilst Mrs Belanov appeared to be swearing at Mr Belanov, she let go of my hand to open the car door.

I just panicked and ran.

I didn't know where I was or where I was going but I wasn't going, anywhere with that awful couple. I ran up the road and round the corner, ignoring the shouts from behind me. I may not be pretty or clever, but I can run fast, and that overweight man and his nasty faced wife would never catch me.

I kept running and turning corners till I found myself on a busy main road. Red buses inched along behind cars and vans and there were crowds of people out doing their Saturday morning shopping. I dodged in and out, certain that no one could catch me. Suddenly, I stumbled head long into two police officers, a policeman and a policewoman. I was terrified. I remembered Maria's words, "The police don't like girls like you. They would lock you up and send you back to Romania".

Laughing, they took hold of my arms and said something I didn't understand. They looked as if they were going to walk on, and certainly didn't look like they wanted to lock me up. On impulse, I thought I might prefer to go back home. I grabbed the policewoman and started jabbering at her in Romanian. She stopped laughing and looking at my tear-stained face and must have realised something was wrong. She tried asking me questions, but I couldn't understand her.

The police officer was talking into his radio, and the policewoman looked into my eyes and pointed at her chest. 'Lucy.'

'Katya.' At least I understood that.

I couldn't stop crying, and Lucy handed me a tissue.

At that moment I saw Mr and Mrs Belanov drive past in their car with Maria leaning out of the window. I shrank back behind Lucy, who looked to see who I was hiding from. She looked at the car and then at me, but when she turned back, the car had disappeared into the traffic.

A police car drove up and Lucy and I climbed in. I bit my lip and stared out of the window. Was I doing the right thing? Maria had said you had to bribe the police, otherwise they might beat you, but at the police station they were very kind. They smiled, and they even gave me something to eat and drink. Despite the kindness and food, my stomach churned, and I clasped my arms around my knees to try to stop them trembling.

I was sitting alone in a corner of a foreign police station – far from home.

Chapter 10

Hours later a Romanian lady called Natasha knocked on the door and peered into the room. I must have dozed off for a little while, but when I heard her voice, I sat up and smiled. Someone spoke Romanian.

'Are you Katya?'

'Yes.'

'I've come to help. The police called me. What happened? Why did you stop the police in the street?' She murmured with her hand on my arm.

I felt tears pricking my eyes, but I took a deep breath and explained what had happened since we left Romania. It was all rather muddled, but Natasha helped me explain.

Finally, I asked her the question that had been troubling me the most.

'I don't have any money for a bribe. Will they beat me?' I whispered.

'Who? The police?' She frowned. 'No. Who told you that?'

'No one.' I looked down at my feet.

'Do you know which house you slept in?' she asked.

'No. I can't remember.'

'Don't worry. We'll find somewhere safe for you.'

I was surprised. Safe from whom? Safe from Mr and Mrs Belanov or the police?

A little later Natasha took me to another house, but as we walked through the front door, my heart sank. In a large room off the hall, about ten young people were watching television and some were playing snooker. I recognised immediately that it was a children's home.

I looked with a mix of horror and disappointment at the other young people. Was this their idea of somewhere safe? Now I was back where I had started but in a foreign country.

'You'll be fine here,' Natasha said, smiling at me.

'I hope so,' I said. 'they don't look friendly.'

Indeed, everyone was looking at me with contempt, and no one was smiling or welcoming. Maria's words rang in my head.

A man spoke to a girl about my age with bright red hair and a silver stud in her nose. She pulled a face and huffed loudly, but she came over and pointed at herself.

'Teresa.'

I tried smiling, but tears were welling up in my eyes again.

'Katya,' I stammered.

'Come.' Teresa beckoned me to follow her down a corridor.

I looked back at Natasha, who waved and smiled before turning to leave. Teresa opened a door to a room with a bed, cupboard, and chair. At least it was clean.

'Thank you.'

'Food,' Teresa pointed to her watch and held 10 fingers out.

I nodded. She left me. I didn't have a watch, so I had no idea how long 10 minutes was, but after a while I went to try to find everyone. They were sitting round tables in the dining room. No one invited me to join them. I crept over to a table and tentatively pulled out a chair with a questioning look on my face. The girls there just grunted at me and carried on with their conversation.

The food was tasty - chicken and chips with ice cream afterwards. I was starving, and I gobbled my food down. Everyone helped stack the plates and clear the tables before going back to watch the television. One member of staff tried speaking to me.

'Katya?' she asked.

I nodded.

I pointed at her and raised my eyebrows.

'Tracey.' She smiled.

'Poland?'

'No. Romania.'

'Oh. How old?'

She held up her fingers, but my limited English from school was coming back to me.

I counted in my head. 'Thirteen,' I said in English.

She smiled. 'Well done.'

Another worker came in the room and clapped their hands. She said something, but I didn't catch it. Everyone groaned and complained, but they turned the television off and started wandering away.

'Bedtime,' Tracey said to me and held her two hands by her cheek.

In bed, I lay for a long time wondering what would happen to me now. Might they send me back to Romania? I would be in awful trouble, but surely it was better than going with Mr and Mrs Belanov?

Katya's Story

Chapter 11

No one spoke to me next morning over breakfast. I tried listening to the conversation, but the young people's English was all too fast for me. Teresa asked me a question, but I didn't understand. She turned to the others and muttered a remark and they all looked at me and sniggered. I blushed.

I was surprised that the young people were allowed to come and go as they pleased. They went out, and I found myself alone. Another member of staff tried to talk to me in very slow, careful sentences. I managed to speak a few more words. With sign language, I asked if I could do anything. I didn't want to sit around all day by myself, so he gave me some jobs to do.

On Monday, Natasha arrived. 'Katya. We're trying to find a school for you. It'll probably take a week.'

It was such a relief to speak Romanian after a weekend of misunderstanding English.

'Really? Won't they send me home?'

'No. No one's sure yet. You'll stay here for a bit.'

The constant fluttering like a caged bird in my stomach eased a little.

'But how will I manage in school? My English is very poor.'

'They'll give you extra lessons. Try listening to everyone here and speak a little English every day.'

Three days later, when everyone had come back from school, they said I could go out with Teresa and her friend to the shops. They even gave me some money. I had been indoors for almost five days, so it was lovely to get out. We walked to a local mall and Teresa and her friend indicated they were leaving me and would meet up again in an hour.

Apprehension churned in my stomach as they left. I wandered along looking in the shop windows. I stopped outside a store selling jewellery, hair bands and bags, wondering if I was brave enough to go in. I certainly would be buying nothing.

Suddenly my arm was grasped in a vice like grip.

'Looking for some pretty things, Katya?' Maria hissed in my ear. 'You should know you can't get away that easily.'

I tried pulling away, but Maria had a very firm hold on me. I was just about to scream when she said, 'Don't. No one cares about girls like you. Look how they left you on your own.'

She pulled on my arm. 'Come along.'

Tears started to roll down my cheeks. I think I may have seen Teresa and her friend in the distance, but they didn't help me.

Maria shoved me into a car and locked the door. Soon we were back at that house, and I was imprisoned in the room with nothing to eat or drink. They even left a bucket. I wasn't allowed to use the bathroom.

Next morning Mr and Mrs Belanov arrived and this time there was no escape. I was driven to a house in a quiet street in another city about two hours away.

'Out,' Mrs Belanov said.

I staggered as she hauled me from the car. I stumbled as I was pushed up a path through an overgrown garden full of weeds and flowers to the front door, with Mrs Belanov gripping my arm.

Paint was peeling off the front door and window frames and the glass was filthy. She pushed me inside and I looked round in revulsion at the dirty state of all the rooms. A musty smell enveloped everything.

Mrs Belanov said something to me in English.

'What did you say?' I asked in Romanian.

'No Romanian.' She pointed round the house. 'Dirty. You clean.'

My eyes started to fill with tears. 'Children?'

'No children. You work. No cry.' She slapped my face.

I stared at her with dismay, putting my hand to my burning face.

'Maria said children.'

'No children.'

She dragged me into the kitchen and opened a cupboard. A vacuum, bucket, mop, cloths, and cleaning fluids fell out. She pointed to them and left me to it. With an aching heart, I took the bucket to the sink, filled it up and began my chores.

My new life in England had begun.

Chapter 12

My life became one of abuse, beatings and silence. I was like a small animal being circled by vicious beasts, never knowing when they might attack. Anxiety gripped me and my stomach responded with cramps and constant upsets. My head thumped with migraines, and I felt nauseous.

Every day was the same. Cleaning and more cleaning. Mr and Mrs Belanov were slobs. They never cleared up anything. In the morning there were all the dirty dishes from the night before waiting for me to start my day. If I cleaned the kitchen, half an hour later it would be covered in their mess again. I had to do everything.

Loneliness sat like a rock in my heart. There was no conversation. They pointed to what I must do and if I did something wrong, I was bombarded with a flood of Russian and often a beating. Every night I was exhausted. The work never ended, and it was never good enough. But I had chosen to come here. It was my fault and I had no one to blame but myself.

If I worked well, I might be allowed to sleep on a bed in a tiny bedroom. Otherwise, I was pushed into a cupboard under the stairs. I never knew what was going to happen. At some point in the evening when I was drooping from fatigue, they would either point upstairs or shove me in the cupboard.

At first, I tried banging on the cupboard door and shouting, but all that earned me was a resounding kick on the door by Mr Belanov's heavy foot. The noise reverberated round the tiny space and made me feel even sicker than normal.

Early on, Mr Belanov pointed at the fridge and cooker and indicated I should cook something.

I shrugged. 'I can't,' I said in English.

He indicated again I must cook something. I tried to remember how to make scrambled eggs, but girls from a home are not taught these things. I made a mess of it and burnt everything. He shouted at me, yanked my hair, and thrust me in the cupboard. After that, Mrs Belanov cooked and I had to clear up after her. I tried to see how she did things in case I had another chance. I just wanted to please them.

They liked to cook enormous meals and then sit and eat them whilst I stood and watched. If there was any left-over, I could stand in the kitchen and eat, but if I wasn't quick enough Mrs Belanov grabbed the plate and put my food in the bin. Often, I was so hungry I took food from the bin.

. I was losing weight. I had always been slender. Now I could see my ribs sticking out on the rare occasion I was allowed a shower. Mrs Belanov would look at me with such disgust in her eyes that I shrank away from her. Then she would hold her nose and point at the bathroom. Shower time. I once tried to use one of the better towels, but I was beaten for that. Mrs Belanov ripped it from my hands and slapped my bare bottom hard. She gave me a tiny tea towel instead.

I wanted to escape, but the house was like a fortress. Doors and windows were locked. Even when I put the rubbish out in the bin by the back door, there was nowhere to go. A high wall and solid gate separated the back from the front of the house. I heard the dustcart each week, but I never put the rubbish by the front gate.

If I did escape, where would I go? I had nowhere to run to and after my experience at the children's home in London, I despaired of ever getting away.

One day, Mrs Belanov grabbed me and thrust my nose into a massive pile of dirty washing. With my arms full of the stinking clothes, I stared at the washing machine trying to work out what to do. Mrs Belanov pointed to the dials and left me to it. I fumbled with the dials and tried to understand what each setting did by the picture beside it. Why was it so complicated? I picked a setting that I hoped would clean the clothes and bedding. I didn't know what to do with the powder, so I just threw some in with the washing and hoped for the best. After the first load was finished, I went and asked Mrs Belanov with sign language where to hang it to dry.

She went through it carefully to make sure it was clean. It seemed to be alright because she thrust the basket into my hands, shoved me hard and unbolted the back door. She indicated a line draped across the wilderness of the garden. I had never been outside for more than a few minutes before - only to put the rubbish in the bin. It was wonderful to breathe in some fresh air, though I had to wade through knee high grass to hang the washing. Flowers were peeping through the grass, and I longed to pick some to bring indoors. A dilapidated glasshouse stood in the corner, with long, trailing, prickly branches winding in and out of the broken panes. A tall hedge of bushes surrounding a wire mesh fence ran along the back of this jungle.

It was whilst I was hanging out some washing, that I heard a crash. I looked up and there was a new ball sized hole in the roof of the glasshouse. I laughed for the first time in months, but my laughter stuck in my throat when two boys appeared at the fence, having pushed through the hedge. They called out to me in English.

I didn't know what they said, but I knew I must disappear - fast. Mr and Mrs Belanov would thrash me if they knew I had talked to anyone. They had made it plain right from the start that speaking to anyone was forbidden.

I raced indoors leaving the rest of the wet washing in the basket and stood panting with my back to the kitchen door. Mrs Belanov fortunately was busy, and Mr Belanov was out. I glanced out of the kitchen window, but the boys had disappeared. I waited till I was certain they had gone and then went and finished hanging out the clothes.

When I came back in, I heard a tapping on the front door. Mr and Mrs Belanov hardly ever had visitors. I wondered what I should do, but Mrs Belanov appeared.

She stood by the door and said nothing.

'Excuse me.' An older boy's voice drifted through the locked door. He said something else which I didn't catch. My stomach churned. If it was the boy whose ball came over the hedge, I was in trouble.

'No. Go away,' Mrs Belanov said.

'Well. Could the girl get the ball and throw it back?'

I wasn't sure what he said till Mrs Belanov's eyes narrowed as she glared at me.

'No girl. Go away.'

Now I was in trouble.

'But we saw her.'

'You're trespassing. Go away.'

I ran into the kitchen and carried on with the washing and cleaning out a cupboard.

Suddenly, Mrs Belanov squeezed my arm. 'Stupid girl. That boy saw you.'

'I couldn't help it.' I tried explaining in Romanian. 'I was hanging the washing out and the ball just came over, but I didn't talk to them. Please.'

She hit my head hard several times with a wooden spoon till I felt blood trickle down my cheek. She looked me right in the eye and let rip a flood of Russian, full of venom.

'I'm sorry.' I said in English, my tears mingling with the blood.

She pushed me into the cupboard so hard that I banged my injured head on the wall.

I was in the dark, alone and injured. Nobody knew or cared.

Chapter 13

It was a full day later before I was allowed out into the light. I was starving and I smelt, but the cupboard stunk even worse. I had had to relieve myself in the corner as I just couldn't wait any longer.

'You shower and then clean there.' Mrs Belanov pointed to the cupboard. She had spoken in Romanian, but again held her nose with a look of repugnance.

I ran upstairs and showered. I stood under the hot water for as long as I dared. Next, I tackled the stinking cupboard, knowing that I would almost certainly be back there soon. I craved something to eat and in one of the kitchen cupboards I found an old piece of bread, which I managed to chew and swallow with difficulty. I even sneaked a bit of cheese from the fridge. I learned early on that stealing food earned a beating. Fortunately, no one came to disturb me.

After that, I was only allowed out of my cupboard in the evening. I had to do all the cleaning during the night. When I did the washing, I hung it on an airing rack in the bedroom. No more going out into the garden.

I had to learn to iron as well. That was very difficult because I had never used an iron before, and I was frightened that I might burn myself. When I was ironing, Mr Belanov liked to come and grab the iron and wave it close to my face.

I could feel the heat, but I did not want to show fear, so I stared back at him. However, that made him mad. He was just about to place the iron on my cheek when I panicked and fled from the room. His mocking laugh followed me.

One morning, when I was putting an enormous pile of ironing away in their bedroom, I walked past the open door of Mr Belanov's office that was next to the bedroom. He was sitting at his computer. On the screen there were pictures of girls. One of them was Serena. I was surprised. I thought Serena was a receptionist. Why was he looking at her picture? I stopped to make certain.

The next pictures were all girls from the home in Romania. Suzie was there parading her new clothes and others I recognised from the journey. It must all be part of Tomas's business. I continued my chores, very puzzled.

It was about this time that Maria re-appeared. I was working in the kitchen when I heard her voice. Mrs Belanov had opened the front door to her and then disappeared into the front room. I ran into the hall with a big smile on my face and I lifted my arms slightly hoping I might be hugged.

Maria was carrying a big, heavy bag. She dropped her bag on the floor and looked at me. Then with a slight smile she opened her arms, and I ran into them. I sighed. Everything was going to be fine. Maria was going to put things right and get me out of here.

She held me at arms' length. 'Well, Katya. Enjoying your new life?'

She glanced at herself in the hall mirror that was sparkling from my cleaning and rearranged a few stray hairs.

'No.'

'Really?' She raised her eyebrows.

'Mr and Mrs Belanov are cruel They beat me and lock me in that cupboard.' I pointed at the space under the stairs. 'I am always cleaning, and nothing is ever good enough. They don't give me food. I hate it here.'

'How ungrateful you sound!' She frowned at me and tutted. 'Your choice to come here. Remember. A lot of girls would be delighted to get a job like this in England.'

'They can come here instead of me. I want to go back to Romania.'

Maria laughed. How could she laugh? How mean. Maria left me to find Mr Belanov who was working upstairs in his office. My shoulders sagged and tears filled my eyes as I returned to my cleaning.

A loud argument with much shouting filled the house and Maria stormed out without a word and without the heavy bag. Maybe she was asking them to be nice to me. I didn't think so. She doesn't care. No one cares. I am just a poor Romanian, stuck here to slave for some horrible people. I would take my life if only I knew how.

A few days later, I was cleaning Mr Belanov's office in the evening. He was downstairs watching television and I saw the big bag that Maria had brought. It was unzipped and I was curious. I quickly peeped inside. There was a pile of dark red passports, wrapped in plastic, that looked brand new and stacks and stacks of what looked like credit cards. I lifted one pack of credit cards and underneath was a thick wodge of money wrapped in a cardboard wrapper. I peered further into the bag and found more packs of notes, mostly Euros but some British pounds and some I didn't recognise at all. Hearing a footstep, I carried on cleaning, but I was baffled.

I didn't know what Mr Belanov did for a living. What would he do that used passports and credit cards? He spent ages on his computer or on the phone. Often his voice was raised. Occasionally someone called at the house, and I would be pushed out of the way into the kitchen or the cupboard. They seemed to mostly speak Russian or English. Occasionally, the conversation was in Romanian. I was puzzled.

However, it was a secret visitor that was about to change things. Once, as I was vacuuming the back room downstairs late at night, I heard a quiet scratching noise that I only just picked up. I stopped to listen, and I saw a hand lightly tapping the outside glass of the garden doors. I had only just cleaned them the night before. I went to look more closely and the boy from the garden next door was crouching down by the doors.

He held up a card that I read slowly. 'ARE YOU OK?' it said.

I shook my head and tried not to weep.

'DO YOU WANT HELP?' the next card said.

I shrugged. I heard footsteps, so I quickly turned the vacuum on again. Mrs Belanov came into the room, sneered at me, and deliberately put her sticky fingers on the clean glass. I tried to ignore her, but anger like a hot volcano welled up inside me.

Later, when I went to put the rubbish in the bin, I lifted the lid and noticed a long string hanging down the back of it. On the end was a little plastic bag with a note. I untied it and quickly stuffed it into my pocket and ran back indoors as Mr Belanov looked out. He snarled something unpleasant at me and hit my head as I scuttled past.

I hoped the note was from the boy. Maybe he could rescue me.

Katya's Story

Chapter 14

I stood at the kitchen sink looking out of the window onto the dark garden and with trembling hands opened the plastic wallet and pulled out the note.

I struggled to read the English words.
IMPORTANT Are you in trouble? Can I help? Simon.

Tears formed in my eyes. I leaned against the sink, taking big gulps of air. Someone might help. I stood trying to work out what to do. Inside the little bag was a pencil and some blank paper. I must write a note back. Maybe Simon would get his parents to help.

I heard a sound behind me and quickly stuffed everything back in my pocket and put my hands in the washing-up bowl.

A hand gripped my arm, already covered in bruises and it felt as if my skin would pop open like an over-ripe plum. Inside I panicked in case he had seen the note, but I kept my face calm. Fear seemed to bring the worst out of the Belanovs. I was dragged into the cupboard and the door slammed behind me. It was too dark to see or do anything, but nothing could stop my thoughts.

I worked out what I would write. I knew I would not be out again till the afternoon and when the morning light seeped into my hole through the cracks round the door, I had just enough light to write a reply.

'My English not good. Bad man and woman keep me here. Want to run away but cannot. They beat me. Please help. Katya.'

I put everything back in the little bag and made sure there was enough string to re-tie it on the dustbin. Then I tucked it into a crack between the cupboard wall and floor. I was terrified they would find it if it was in my pocket. In here, my note was safe.

When I was let out, I did all the chores, the cleaning, washing, and ironing but inside a little bird of hope fluttered.

Late in the evening I put the black bag by the back door ready to go to the bin and tiptoed to retrieve my note. As I put the black bag into the bin, I quickly tied my note on the hinge and let the string hang down the back. I hoped the Belanovs would not come out and see it.

I ran indoors and locked the door behind me. Mrs Belanov pointed up the stairs. My heart sank. What had I forgotten or what horrible task would she demand I do? I kept my face composed but sniffed at her with contempt. I was slapped for that, but it was worth it for I was tired of being pushed around by these slobs. I may have to do their dirty work, but I would not show them fear no matter how terrified I felt. Hope gave me courage.

Surprisingly, Mrs Belanov pushed me into the small bedroom. No cupboard tonight. I walked past her with my head held high as if it was my right to sleep here. I thought she might change her mind, but with a smack on my head, she turned around and left me. I lay down on a bed for the first time in weeks.

Despite my feelings of optimism that I might escape, exhaustion overcame me, and I slept.

Katya's Story

Chapter 15

For two days and nights, I heard nothing. I continued my lonely, domestic nightmare - always cleaning, clearing up, washing, ironing. Mrs Belanov even started speaking to me in Romanian instead of just pointing. Maybe Maria had said something. But this miserable existence was so harsh that I longed for my unhappy life in the Romanian home. At least in that place, there were girls my age to speak to. At least there were babies who loved me whom I could cuddle. At least I had a bed to sleep on every night and three meals a day.

That night, Mr Belanov had some old furniture he wanted to put out by the bin. I helped him carry out a table and some chairs. He went indoors and I picked up the nightly black bag to pop in the bin. As I did, so someone grabbed my hand.

'Come on, Katya!'

I stared horrified at Simon.

'What?'

'Come on.' He kept pulling me. 'We must run.'

I started to follow him through the wilderness of the garden, tripping over plants and bushes.

I never thought he would try and rescue me himself. I thought he would get an adult to come and demand to speak to Mr and Mrs Belanov. They might persuade my employers to let me go back to Romania.

At that moment Mr Belanov looked out to see where I was.

He roared at me in Romanian, 'Katya! Come back. Now.'

I stopped. This was not how it was meant to be.

'Hurry.' Simon continued to yank my hand, but fear brought me to a standstill.

Mr Belanov raced up the garden, surprising me by how fast such a big man could move. He sprinted past me, crashing through the undergrowth, and grabbed Simon.

'Get indoors.' He almost spat at me.

I wanted to run but where could I go? I turned and waded back to the house.

Simon started to yell, but Mr Belanov clamped his hand round his mouth and hauled him indoors. He kicked me through the door and yelled for Mrs Belanov who came running.

There was a terrible shouting match between them. I was shoved into the cupboard, but I stuck my ear to the door to try to listen to what was going on. What would they do with Simon? Why had the stupid boy tried to rescue me himself?

There was a lot of banging and crashing and I was terrified that they might harm or even kill Simon. At last, the cupboard door opened, and I was dragged out and my hands squeezed behind my back and tied. Mrs Belanov stuffed an old rag into my mouth and secured it with a tightly bound scarf.

I caught a glimpse of Simon tied to a kitchen chair, blood dripping down his face, and gagged. I was lugged out to the car and thrown into the open boot. A minute later Simon landed on top of me. He grunted something and we both rearranged ourselves in the tight space, so we didn't have our feet in each other's mouths.

I heard car doors slamming and then we drove off. I couldn't imagine where they were taking us, but at least there were two of us now. Together might we escape?

Chapter 16

The sounds of traffic seeped into our cramped space for quite a while, but gradually all went quiet. The car stopped and the boot lid opened, and Mr Belanov hauled Simon out. Next, I was yanked from the boot, bumping my shins in the process, and was dumped on the ground.

I looked at our surroundings. The car was parked on a track in a forest and by the track stood a derelict house, all boarded up. Simon and I were half herded, half dragged into the house. Autumn leaves created a crunching carpet as our feet scraped along the ground.

The front door had a padlock on it that Mr Belanov opened and heaved us inside. The smell of damp and neglect was terrible. Mr Belanov opened another door with steps inside leading down into the darkness of a cellar. We were both pushed, tumbling down the wooden stairs, and Mr and Mrs Belanov walked down behind us. They had a torch, and the light showed us a small dingy room with no other door and only small windows high up on one wall. Mr Belanov ripped our gags off our mouths and untied our hands.

'No way out. Don't try shouting for help. No one will hear you.'

Simon spat at Mr Belanov but missed. He smashed his fist into Simon's mouth. Blood from a split lip trickled down his chin. Simon may be stupid, but he is brave. They left us there in the dark and I heard the door at the top of the stairs being locked. I started to weep. Everything hurt. My head, elbow and knees had all been banged in our helter-skelter descent down the stairs. What would happen now?

'Don't cry,' Simon said. 'I'm sorry I messed up.'

I wasn't sure I understood the words, but I knew what he meant.

'Why they take you?' I asked.

'Dunno. Where do you come from?'

'Romania.' My eyes were adjusting to the dark, and I could just make Simon out. He had a kind face, though his lip was swollen and bleeding.

'How long have you been here?'

I shook my head. 'I don't know. A year?'

'Why? You're so young. Why those people?' He frowned in bewilderment.

'No parents. New life. I didn't know ...'

'Hmph. Not much of a life.'

I shrugged. My English may not be very good, but I could understand these simple questions and it was good to talk to someone who wasn't being nasty to me.

'Why you come for me?' I asked.

He smiled. 'When I saw you. In the garden.' He spoke slowly and carefully. 'When we came to the house. To get our ball. That woman said there was no girl.'

I nodded.

'But I saw you. You looked like my sister.'

I smiled.

'Couldn't just leave you.'

'Thank you.'

We both lay down on the cement floor to try to get some sleep. We heard a car driving off. We made ourselves as comfortable as we could and dozed.

Light woke us as it seeped through the grubby windows high up on one wall. We stretched, and I smiled at Simon who grinned back at me, his eyes twinkling. He ran his fingers through his curly hair and scratched his head.

'Morning,' he said.

'Good morning. You hurt?' I was looking at his face, which was bloodstained and bruised. His bottom lip was puffed up and looked very sore.

'A bit. I wonder.' He stood up and went and looked at the window. Simon was quite tall, but it was over his head and with nothing to stand on, it was impossible to do anything.

We heard the door at the top of the steps unlocking, and Mr Belanov appeared with some water and bread.

'No escape.' He sneered at us. 'Your father – foolish man.'

A look of anger and disbelief crossed Simon's face. I didn't understand the conversation then, but Simon explained it to me afterwards.

Simon's disappearance had been on all the local television and radio news programmes. Mr Belanov had contacted his father and demanded a ransom – a big ransom Simon said. He was furious.

'Now we know why they took me. I thought it was because they didn't want anyone to come and find you.'

'No one care about me. People like them terrible,' I said.

94

Simon nodded. Our hands had been re-tied behind our backs after the food, but suddenly Simon looked down his leg.

'My phone,' he said. 'My phone's in my sock!'

Chapter 17

Simon! Simon!' a woman's voice screamed into the silence. 'Are you alright? Where are you?'

I had managed to retrieve Simon's phone from his sock and between us we had turned it on and found his mother's number.

'I'm OK, Mum.' Simon's voice shook. 'They kidnapped me.'

I could see tears glistening on his cheeks.

'Where are you?'

The cellar door banged open and heavy footsteps hurtled down the stairs. Mr Belanov burst into the room and quickly stamped on the phone and Simon's hand. He screamed in pain.

'You moron. That flippin' hurts.'

'Ransom – doubled.'

Mr Belanov turned and stomped away. We heard the cellar door shut.

Simon's face crumpled with disappointment and tears filled his eyes. He was shaking his fingers to try to ease the pain.

'Sorry. Didn't work.'

'Never mind.'

I wriggled over to try to stroke his fingers that were swelling rapidly. One was at a funny angle.

'Do you have mother and father?'

'Yeah. And my sister. Bit younger than me.'

His face looked so warm as he spoke of his family that I felt a stab of jealousy.

'You go to same school?'

'Nope. Different ones.'

'You like school?'

'Not bad. What about you?'

His face was beginning to relax.

'I don't like school. I'm not very clever. School is hard for me.'

Simon smiled and his eyes were sympathetic.

'Who was the other boy? When I first saw you?' I asked.

'What?'

'When the ball broke the glass.'

Simon laughed.

'That was my pal, Chris. We were playing cricket in the garden.'

'I don't understand cricket. I like gymnastics.'

Simon cheered up as we chatted as best we could about the ordinary things of our lives.

Soon after we heard a car arrive and there was much loud shouting between Mr and Mrs Belanov. Moments later the cellar door opened, and our gags were stuffed back into our mouths, and we were dragged up the stairs and back into the car boot.

It was a longer journey this time, and after a while we started to hear more and more traffic noise – cars, lorries and buses. I thought I heard a train rush by. It was obvious we were in a bigger town or city, and Simon started to kick on the boot lid. The car stopped suddenly, and the boot lid was eased open a crack.

'Shut up or I kill you.'

Mr Belanov glared in at us. His face was a mask of hatred and anger.

I shivered, but Simon just stared back at him. I prodded Simon with my foot to stop him from angering Mr Belanov further. I was sure he was capable of killing. The boot lid slammed shut, and our journey continued.

Soon the car stopped and as Simon went to kick the boot lid again, I stopped him and grunted 'No' through the gag. Simon snorted, but put his foot down. Nothing happened. It became hotter and hotter in the confined space, and I was desperate for air.

When I thought I would pass out, the boot lid opened a little and Mr Belanov made a cutting motion across his throat.

'Keep quiet.'

He picked Simon up like a parcel and ran up some steps into a house. He shortly came back for me. I was dumped in a small room with Simon. With a sinking heart, I realised we were back in the house in London. I started to cry as he removed our gags.

'Cry all you like. No one can hear you.' He called me a horrible name in Romanian as he slammed out the door, locking it behind him.

'Why are you crying, Katya?' Simon asked.

'I have been here before. I don't like it.'

'I've no intention of staying here a minute longer than I have to. We're getting out.'

'What?'

'Escape.'

'How?'

I looked at him wide eyed in amazement. It was all very well for him to escape. He had a home and parents to go to. They would just shove me back in a children's home until Maria found me again.

'I don't know yet, but we will escape.'

Chapter 18

A little while later, the door opened, and Maria came in carrying a tray with some bread, cheese, and water.

'What a nuisance you are being, Katya,' she said in Romanian.

'You shouldn't have put me with those nasty people.'

'You wanted to work in England. Remember?'

'Not with slobs like them.'

'That is not a very kind way to talk about Mr and Mrs Belanov who have given you a new home and life.'

She gripped my arm, and her eyes were hard as she clicked her tongue in annoyance.

She looked at Simon.

'At least we may make some money out of you.'

'What did she say?' Simon glared at Maria.

Maria repeated what she had said, but this time in English.

'My father can't pay a ransom.'

'You'll be stuck here then. He'll change his mind when we start cutting off your ear or fingers.' She laughed in that cruel way of hers. 'Eat up.'

She untied our hands and we guzzled down the water and then tried to swallow the hard bread and cheese. I soon gave up and indicated to Simon to eat mine. My appetite was so small these days, but he was glad of the extra food.

Afterwards, we were taken one at a time to the tiny, dirty bathroom. It smelt even worse than the last time I had been here.

Maria wrinkled her nose. 'We will have to get you cleaning round here, won't we, Katya?'

I was tired of her unkindness, so I looked at her contemptuously and spat on the floor. Her face hardened and she hit me hard on the side of my head with her bare fist, her ring scratching my cheek. It hurt, but I managed a laugh.

Simon chuckled when I mimed what had happened.

In reply, he mimed that he wanted us to escape. I shook my head, 'No'. Simon nodded vigorously and inspected the bonds on my wrists that Maria had re-fastened. He turned around so I could see his wrists. They were bound with a thin plastic strip. He tried to pull his hands apart, but they were held fast.

'Your rope is elastic,' he said, indicating my cord might stretch.

I hadn't noticed before, but I wriggled my hands a little apart. He was right. My bonds did stretch a bit. My wrists are tiny, and I don't expect Maria noticed the rope wasn't tight when she put it back on. I kept working away and eventually I twisted one hand free, and the rope slipped off the other.

Simon was elated. 'Mine are not the same,' he said with a frown on his face.

'No. Yours is plastic.'

'Key. Pocket. Sharp.' He nodded down at his pocket. I fumbled in and found a key. It did have a sharp edge and I started sawing away at the thin plastic. It took ages, but finally, as Simon kept pulling his wrists apart, drawing blood, it snapped.

'Now. How are we going to get out?'

He ran over to the door and rattled the handle, but it was locked.

'No surprises there.'

'What?'

'Never mind.'

He looked all around the floor then inspected the ceiling, but there was nothing. He pointed to the window.

We eased up the old-fashioned window and peered out. Our room was three storeys up, too far to jump or even call to the people below. We were more likely to alert someone to our escape. There was a tiny balcony outside the window with a knee-high wall running round it. Simon started to climb out, but I stopped him.

'No. Let me.'

I was slight and I may not have been very bright, but I did have good balance. I stepped out onto the tiny balcony that was barely wide enough for my shoe. I daren't look down. To my right and left there were two more windows both with the little balcony. The window to the left looked shut tight, but the one to the right was slightly open.

'I go there.' I pointed to the window.

'Let me,' Simon said.

'No. I go.'

I stood on the edge of the balcony, balancing with my hand on the wall. My stomach churned and I dared not look down. I could hear the traffic rumbling below and smell exhaust fumes. Voices floated up to me. It was a normal day in London. Would this be my day of escape?

Taking a deep breath, I stepped across. It was further than I thought, and I almost missed the edge. I stumbled slightly and dropped onto the next balcony, my heart racing.

I turned round and saw that Simon had climbed out onto the balcony. He gave me a thumbs-up sign and pointed to the open window. I peered inside. It was a bedroom with a large bed, but no people. I returned Simon's thumbs-up and eased up the window, making sure it made no noise.

I climbed in and Simon landed on the balcony behind me. I looked around the room. The bed was unmade with purple, silky looking sheets, all rumpled. There was hardly any other furniture in the room and a sickly-sweet smell hung in the air. I felt very uncomfortable, but I didn't know why.

'Flip.'

Simon had climbed in behind me and looked round. He wrinkled up his nose.

'This room stinks.'

He tiptoed over to the door, eased it open and looked out into the corridor, and then hurriedly shut it again.

'Someone's coming.'

We looked around, panic-stricken. There was nowhere to hide. The bed was solid, and the only other furniture was a wooden chair and a small table. However, there was a key in the lock. Simon quietly turned it.

No one tried to come in. The footsteps passed, but we heard the door to our old room being unlocked. Any minute now, they were going to discover we had gone. We heard a shout.

'Quick! We must get out.'

He tried to lift the carpet, but it was stuck down all round the edge. I was looking around and panicking. I glanced upwards and saw a small hatch in the ceiling.

'Look!' I pointed.

'How are we going to get up there?'

The door handle rattled.

'Are you in there? Katya! Katya! Answer me.' Maria yelled.

Simon put his finger to his mouth and shook his head. Tears formed in my eyes, my heart was pounding, and my hands shook. Surely if they found us, they would kill me if not Simon.

He stared at me, willing me to stop trembling. He put the only chair on the bed and pointed for me to get up on it. I scrambled up whilst Simon held it steady. There was a loud thud on the door. Someone was trying to break it down.

'Hurry!' Simon whispered.

I wasn't tall enough. Simon grabbed the table and put that on the bed and indicated I should climb up on it. He held the table and passed me the chair and pointed at the hatch. I thrust the chair upwards and dislodged the square piece of wood.

'Quick. Stand the chair on the table.'

I balanced the chair on the table, and Simon helped me climb up onto it. Now I was tall enough to just reach up and get my fingers round the edge of the hole. I pulled myself up. I pushed the hatch clear with my back and turned round to help Simon.

The chair on the table wobbled terribly with no one to hold it. Simon held his hand high and by leaning out I managed to grab hold of his wrist. He almost pulled me back down onto to the bed, but my foot caught round a rafter, and I held onto him.

With his other hand, he clutched hold of the rim of the hatch. He kicked the chair away, and as I hauled on his jersey, he got his elbows onto the floor of the attic and scrambled through the opening. Another loud crash on the door echoed round the bedroom.

I was panic-stricken that we had made a terrible mistake, but Simon must have seen the look on my face because he patted my arm and smiled. We replaced the hatch and looked round. It was very dark, but some light filtered through the roof tiles. We were standing on a few boards, but the rest of the attic was unboarded. Boxes and suitcases were piled haphazardly, and we quickly lugged them on top of the hatch.

'Katya! Katya! Are you up there?' Maria's voice floated up.

'I'll get the silly bitch.' A man's voice growled in Romanian.

I shivered. It was Mr Belanov.

'Come on.' Simon pulled my arm. 'This way.'

He pointed at the rafters and indicated I should only step on them and not on the plaster between them. We tiptoed across the beams till we came to a low wall. We climbed over it and treading on more beams, we soon came to a solid brick wall with no way around it.

We re-traced our steps and stopped by the pile of boxes and suitcases weighting the hatch down. They were wobbling alarmingly as someone was attempting to push the hatch open. I started to cry. My stomach hurt, my head ached, and I felt sick. Simon grabbed my hand and pulled me the other way.

Again, we climbed over a low wall and again a solid brick wall towered over us. There was no way out. We were trapped.

Chapter 19

Tears dripped down my face and my hands shook. Simon grabbed them and looked me in the eye.

'Stop!'

He dropped my hands and put his palms on the wall and started to feel along it. Then he pointed at me and indicated that I should do the same in the opposite direction. I took a deep breath and started to feel along the wall, both high and low. At the far end, right down where the slope of the roof met the floor, there was a gap. The hole was not very big, but big enough.

'Simon!'

I pointed at the hole. He leapt over the beams and peered down.

'Quick! Go!'

A terrible crash behind us indicated they were breaking through the hatch. I stopped and stared wide-eyed back the way we had gone. Simon shook me.

'Go!'

'But …'

'Go!'

He pointed at the tiny hole. I bobbed down and crawled through the opening. Would it be big enough for Simon? His head followed my feet through the hole, but just as his body squeezed through, he stuck. He pointed to his back. I felt along it and found his jersey had caught on a splinter. I ripped it loose. He was almost through when he stopped and started sliding backwards.

I heard Mr Belanov swearing at him, and Simon was shouting back.

'Let go!'

There was a thud and suddenly Simon shot through the hole and scrambled upright.

'I kicked him.'

He indicated with his foot that he had hit him right in his face. I laughed nervously.

'Katya! Come back now or I kill you.' Mr Belanov's voice shouted through the hole.

I could see Simon wanted to kick him through the hole, but I restrained him.

'Don't.'

We tiptoed over the beams in the attic of what must be next-door's house. The roof here had a small window in it which shed a little light, but it did not stop me from falling over a ladder attached to the beams next to what looked like another hatch. I rubbed my bruised shins.

Simon examined the hatch and tried to lift it, but there was no handle.

'Let me.'

I pushed him aside and felt round the edge. It was very rough, but I managed to push my nail under one side and raise it enough for Simon to get his fingers round the wood and lift it clear.

He looked down the hole and then at me. I pointed at the ladder, but he shook his head and indicated I should just drop through the hole. I looked down. It didn't seem too far. I slid down till I was hanging through the opening and then dropped lightly to the floor. Simon followed.

We stared up at the open hatch, half expecting Mr Belanov to glare down at us. Simon gave a nervous laugh as we looked at our new surroundings.

We were standing on a landing with 5 doors off it, some open and some closed. We glimpsed empty rooms through the open doors and peered round them to investigate. Some were storerooms filled with a collection of boxes and debris, and one was completely empty. The end room was lined with dirty kitchen cupboards and an old, stained sink, but none had any means of escape. At the very end of the corridor was another door - locked.

I was trying not to cry, but I was terrified that we were imprisoned here. Would they find us? Simon looked down from the front windows to the street below and pointed out Maria walking slowly along looking up at each building. I shrank back from the window. Simon ran and looked out of the back windows. I followed, and below we could see overgrown gardens and scruffy back yards filled with rubbish.

To our right though, was a metal fire escape zigzagging down the wall. It passed right by the kitchen window. We rushed back and leaning across the sink, tried to lift the dirty window, but it was stuck. Then we noticed that in our panic we had missed the catch. It was rusty, but we tugged it back, and the window creaked open. Just as we were about to climb over the sink and step onto the metal fire escape, a shrill alarm went off.

'Damn!' Simon shouted as he crawled out the window. 'Come on'.

I climbed out after him and we ran down the fire escape as fast as we could. Halfway down, an old man looked out of a window at us and banged on the glass as we went by.

At the bottom was an old blue door which, without warning burst open, nearly knocking us over, and the man rushed out.

'Oi! What are you doing?'

He tried to grab us, but Simon pushed him, and he staggered backwards.

We ran down the yard, jumping over all sorts of rubbish towards a brick wall at the end with the man pursuing us. Simon leapt up onto some boxes heaped against the wall and vaulted over it. He let out a yell as he flew over. I followed on behind and realised why he had yelled. There was broken glass along the top of the wall. I stuck my hand into a sharp piece and winced as I landed in an alley behind. Blood dripped from both our hands, and I sucked my cut finger.

The old man looked over the wall at us and let out a flood of words that I did not understand.

Simon held up his hands. 'Sorry.'

We were about to run down the alley to the road at the bottom when Mr Belanov appeared, standing hands on hips, breathing fast and blocking our way. We turned around, but a delivery van was parked wall to wall in the alley behind us. We were cornered.

Chapter 20

With a roar, Mr Belanov raced towards us.

'Katya! Run!'

Simon pushed me away.

'No. You must come too.'

I grabbed his hand, but he shook me free.

'Please, Katya. Go. Now.'

I started to run towards the van though, I hated to leave Simon behind, but maybe if I escaped, I could get help. I jumped up on the bonnet of the van and onto the roof as I heard a terrible crash. I turned round to look. Mr Belanov and Simon were both lying tangled on the ground in a mass of stinging nettles. Simon must have blocked his way somehow.

Mr Belanov cursed terribly. He hauled Simon to his feet and pinned him up against a fence. With his hands around his throat, he started to choke him. I could hear Simon coughing and spluttering.

I started to climb back down to run and help him though I had no idea what I could do against Mr Belanov. At that

119

moment Maria appeared and ran and grabbed Mr Belanov's arm and yelled at him to let go.

'He's worthless if you kill him. You idiot.'

Breathing heavily and with a terrible look on his face, Mr Belanov released Simon.

'Go. Get her.' Maria pointed at me. 'Before she causes any more trouble.'

He turned to glower at me and with more cursing, hurtled towards the van. I clambered back on the vehicle roof and jumped down the back into the alley. It was muddy and tripping over the litter and weeds, I sprinted as fast as I could to get away from trouble.

Mr Belanov jumped up onto the van roof and then leapt down into the alley to chase me. I was not as quick as I used to be. Months of no proper food and imprisonment had made me weak. I could hear him catching me up.

'You stop now, you little madam.' His breath came in great gasps. 'I'll kill you with my bare hands. I'll tear your arms and legs off. You'll regret the day you ran away.'

Fear kept me moving. At the end of the alley, was another long road of houses with cars parked along the kerb. Not knowing where to go, I turned left and continued running

along the pavement. A lady was walking her dog and I ran up
to her and tried explaining that I was running away from - I
turned around - him. I pointed at Mr Belanov who slowed
down, still panting, and walked up to the lady.

'She has been very naughty,' he said in English, smiling
and trying to grab my arm. 'She needs to come with me.'

'No!' I screamed. 'Bad man.'

The lady's dog, though small, was growling at him.

I hid behind the lady yelling, 'No. No.'

'I'm not sure she should go with you,' the lady said.

'She must come with me. I am her father.' Mr Belanov's
face was getting redder and angrier.

'No. No father. Bad man.'

'I think I should call the police,' the lady said, fumbling in
her bag for her phone.

Suddenly, Mr Belanov pushed the lady so hard she fell
over. The dog started yapping at him, but he kicked it and it
yelped in pain.

I just ran. As fast as I could, I sprinted down the road. Turning a corner, I saw a pile of rubbish by a wheelie bin in a front garden. I dashed into the garden and ducked down quickly behind the bin and squeezed into the gap between it and the house. I eased some rubbish bags towards me to conceal my hiding place.

I heard Mr Belanov race down the road and then stop. More muttered curses. He turned round and walked back down the road towards me. I peeped out from my hiding place. He was looking in every front garden.

'Katya? Katya? Where are you?' His voice was low but full of menace.

I curled up as small as possible into my space and cowered down. I daren't look out, but surely, he could hear my pounding heart? It echoed loudly in my ears.

I heard his heavy breathing and snarling as he walked past. Then all went silent. I didn't know what to do. Should I stay or run? After a little while, when I had heard nothing, I peered out. The street was quiet, and I couldn't see anyone. I crept out of my hiding place and tiptoed into the street.

With a bellow, Mr Belanov started flying down the road towards me.

'I knew if I waited long enough you would come out, you little madam.'

At that moment a police car came screaming round the corner, lights flashing and sirens wailing. Mr Belanov stopped in his tracks and turned around and sauntered off down the road, but the lady with the dog must have been waiting.

'That's him.' She shouted to the policemen as he got out of the car. She pointed at Mr Belanov as he speeded up his walk.

'Excuse me, sir. Could we have a word?' the police officer said.

Mr Belanov started to jog, and the police officer ran after him.

I just stood there. The tension I had been feeling popped like a balloon and I burst into tears and started crying and crying.

'There, there, dear,' the lady with the dog said, patting my arm.

Having started, I just couldn't stop. I sobbed and sobbed, and tears poured down my face until I couldn't breathe. I started gasping and there was a terrible tightness in my throat. I felt as if I was choking.

The lady with the dog stared at me with great concern.

'You need to do something,' she said to the other police officer.

'I've called an ambulance.'

I sat down on the ground, gulping. The dog, sensing my misery, came and licked my tears. I was breathless and panting, but his rasping tongue almost made me laugh. I stroked the little dog who only licked me more.

I didn't notice the ambulance arrive till a lady paramedic was kneeling beside me, taking my pulse and asking me questions. I looked at her blankly and carried on stroking the dog.

'I don't think she's English,' the lady with the dog said.

'Come.'

The paramedic pointed at the ambulance, but I shrunk away from her.

'It's alright, dear,' the dog lady said.

Her eyes were reassuring, and she nodded at me.

'I'm Pam. Shall Trixie and I come too?'

I nodded. She helped me stand, picked up the dog, took my arm and came with me into the ambulance.

I don't know whether the paramedics wanted to have a dog in the ambulance, but no one said anything. Pam put Trixie next to me and I continued to stroke her, and my breathing became easier. I stopped feeling as if I would choke and I almost stopped crying.

The paramedics did some tests, and everything must have been alright though they looked carefully at some of my cuts and bruises. Eventually they took me back to the police car, but Mr Belanov was sitting there. I saw he was wearing handcuffs.

I started to cry again and turned to run away, but Pam took my arm and hung on tight.

'Ssh. Don't worry.'

She muttered something to the police officer who led us away from that car to another police car parked across the street.

'They're taking you to the police station. Shall I come too?' she asked.

I nodded and together we all got into the back of the police car.

Suddenly I remembered Simon. What had they done with him?

'Simon! Where's Simon?'

I tried to climb out of the police car, but the doors must have been locked. I banged on the windows.

'Who's Simon?' Pam asked.

'Friend. Bad man take him.'

There was a hurried conversation between Pam and the police. The police officer got out of the car and brought a policewoman over who came and sat in the front of the car. It was Lucy. I sighed with relief, but I could not stop shaking and tears continued to drip down my face.

Lucy smiled at me. 'Hello. Again. What happened?'

It was all too much. I started to sob and sob, and I just poured out my story in Romanian. Lucy patted my hand and said something, and Pam gave me a squeeze.

'Police station,' she said.

I nodded to show I understood.

Chapter 21

S imon. Must find Simon.'

I kept going on and on to anyone who would listen. I was back in the same room at the police station, but this time with Pam and Trixie. We sat round a wooden table on the only three chairs.

'Yes. Yes. Don't worry.'

Pam and Lucy tried to reassure me, but I was worried sick.

'Bad people got Simon.'

'Where, Katya?' Lucy asked.

'House.'

'Where?'

I shook my head. How could I tell them? I hoped Natasha or someone who spoke Romanian would come soon.

'Is it near here, dear?' Pam asked.

I nodded. 'Yes. Close.'

Another lady brought three mugs of tea on a tray into the room and set it on the table. Pam shovelled heaps of sugar in one mug and passed it to me. I sipped it but winced at the sugary taste. We never had that much sugar in our tea in Romania.

'Simon. They must find Simon.'

Trixie had been sitting on the floor, but she jumped up at my legs. I picked her up and stroked her silky ears. It was so soothing.

There was a knock on the door and a police officer opened it and showed a lady into the room. It was Maria, all smiles.

I jumped up, dropping Trixie, and backed away.

'There you are, Katya. What a lot of trouble you have been causing.'

She spoke quietly and kindly in Romanian. I hid behind Lucy.

'No. No.'

'This lady says she is responsible for you here,' the police officer said. 'She has come to collect you.'

Maria held out her hand to me. 'Come along.'

'I am not going anywhere with you,' I said to Maria in Romanian.

'I think you will. No one will believe a Romanian orphan.'

'Where's Simon?'

'Who?' She laughed, that unnatural little sound. 'Are you making up more stories?'

She then said something to the others in the room in English. They all stared at her uncertainly.

At that moment there was another knock on the door and Natasha popped her head round it.

'Oh. Hello. I am so pleased to see you,' I said in Romanian. 'They must find Simon. Maria wants to take me away, but I don't want to go with her. Do I have to?'

Natasha spoke to the two police officers in the room, and they asked Maria something. She glared at me as the police officer escorted her out. I sighed and my heartbeat started to slow down. I almost began to cry again.

'Simon. They must rescue Simon.'

'Tell us who Simon is, Katya,' Natasha said.

'He tried to rescue me, but they kidnapped him. Mr Belanov asked his father for money. They said if he didn't pay, they would cut off his ears or toes.'

Natasha translated this into English and Lucy looked at her, then me and jumped up.

'Excuse me,' she said and raced out of the room.

'Where has she gone?' I asked.

'To get Simon I should think. The police must have been looking for him. Is he the boy that has been on all the news?'

'I don't know. Is he?'

'He disappeared from his house a few days ago. Everyone has been concerned for his safety. It wasn't like him to leave home.'

'That must be him. He is very brave.'

Lucy reappeared and spoke to Natasha.

'They want you to come in a police car and see if you can show them the house. Can you do that?'

I nodded. 'I think so.'

'Do you want me and Trixie to come too, or can you manage now?' Pam asked.

I turned to Natasha.

'Please tell Pam I think I will be fine now that you have arrived. Please thank her. She has been so kind.'

Natasha told her what I had said. Pam smiled and patted my arm and held Trixie for me to stroke one last time.

'Thank you,' I said.

'That's alright, dear.'

Lucy and Natasha took me to the back of the police station where there were three or four police cars. A police officer was waiting for us in the driver's seat and Lucy sat next to him while Natasha and I got into the back.

'Where's Maria?' I asked Natasha.

'At the police station. They asked her to wait while we interviewed you further. She took quite a risk coming to get you.'

'Why?'

'I think she was hoping to get to you before you told the police what had been happening. Before you told them about Simon. If we had linked her to Simon, we could have arrested her.'

I was struggling to understand.

The police car pulled out into traffic and after a short way drove down a side street, but it was unfamiliar. At the bottom, we turned right and then right again. The streets and houses all looked the same. I peered out anxiously as we drove up and down. Suddenly I saw something.

'Stop! That is the end of the alley where I met Pam with her dog.'

I recognised the alley, and I could see the van parked up it.

'There. That van. I jumped over it. Mr Belanov followed. Can I get out, please?'

Lucy opened the door and Natasha and I climbed out. I walked slowly up the alley, looking at the backs of the houses. Most of the backyards had walls, fences or even garages, so it was difficult to see the houses, but occasionally there was a gate or a gap in the fence.

'There. We ran down there.'

I pointed at a fire escape snaking down the back wall of a house and at the bottom was the blue door where the man had popped out.

'Which house did you come from, Katya? That one?' Lucy asked.

'No.'

I tried to work out how far we had come in the attics, but it was very hard. Was it to the right or the left of the house with the fire escape?

'Shall we go back to the car? We know which road now?' Natasha said, translating.

We walked back to the car, and I looked around before climbing in. Suppose Pam had not been walking Trixie when I ran out of the alley. What might have happened? I shivered. The police officer drove us round the corner, and I gazed at all the houses.

'That's Mr Belanov's car.'

I pointed to a white car parked at the side of the road. Suddenly I ducked down.

'Tomas is by that black sports car,' I hissed.

Natasha translated.

'Who's Tomas?'

'He runs the businesses. Maria works with him.'

'Which house, Katya?' Lucy asked.

I peeped round Natasha and saw Tomas staring at the police car as we drove slowly by. I bobbed down again.

'The one with the open front door.'

Lucy spoke urgently into the little radio on the front of her uniform, and the police car sped off down the street.

'We're taking you back to the police station. You will be safe there.'

I clung onto Natasha. 'What about Maria? Will I have to go with her?'

'No. Maria has left.'

'Why?'

'She wanted to go. She had done nothing we could arrest her for – yet.'

'Maria can be nice. But she tricked me. She said she had a job for me looking after children. Mr and Mrs Belanov have no children. They are cruel, too.'

Natasha squeezed my shoulders. 'You can tell me all about it in a minute.'

The police car swung into the back of the police station. Many policemen in black uniform with helmets and guns were gathering. We hurried inside back to the now familiar room.

'Will they get Simon?'

I shivered and clung onto Natasha. Lucy had come back into the room.

'Hopefully,' she said. 'They are going soon now. While we wait, why don't you tell us what happened since we last saw you.'

'Maria found me when we went out shopping from that children's home. She took me back to the London place. Mr and Mrs Belanov then drove me to their house.'

I started to cry again.

'They were very unkind. I had to clean all the time. They beat me and kept me in a cupboard, and I was always hungry.'

I kept sniffing, so Natasha handed me a tissue and I blew my dripping nose. I continued my story of how Simon had appeared and tried to rescue me.

'Silly boy. I thought he would get his parents to help. Not rescue me himself.'

I smiled as I remembered his bravery.

I told them both how Mr Belanov had kidnapped Simon and then tried to hide us in that ruined house in the forest.

'Simon remembered his phone, but when he called his mother, Mr Belanov stamped on the phone and his hand. It was very painful.'

'We found that house after you had gone because we traced the phone signal,' Lucy said. 'We even found the smashed phone, so we knew Simon had been there, but we didn't know how or why he had been kidnapped.'

'They took us back to London and that house, but Simon wanted to escape.'

I explained how we had climbed into the bedroom next door and up into the attic and then down through the other house and into the alley where Mr Belanov had cornered us.

'Simon told me to run. He must have stopped Mr Belanov. He was so angry he tried to choke him to death. Maria stopped him and took Simon away. I don't know where. Mr Belanov chased me down the alley. Till I bumped into Pam.'

There was a knock at the door and a police officer stuck his head into the room and said something to Lucy. She smiled at me.

'Come. I have someone you must meet.'

I was so fearful that Maria had come back for me. Lucy took me down the corridor to another room and opened the door. Sitting on a chair wrapped in a blanket was Simon. In the corner, a police officer was standing, watching.

With a cry, I rushed into the room and hugged him.

'Katya.'

He burst into tears and so did I.

Chapter 22

Simon looked awful. His face was white, so pale, and there were dark circles under his eyes. His lips were swollen, and he had bruises on his cheek and a cut above his eye. There were red marks round his neck and one hand was misshapen, red, and puffed up.

'They found you.' I said, staring at his appearance.

'Yeah.'

'How?'

'Police came. Broke in. Rescued me.'

'Maria?'

'Got her.'

'Tomas?'

'Who?'

'Boss man.'

Simon shrugged. 'Dunno.' His face brightened. 'Loads of girls.'

'What?'

'Girls. Like you.'

'Where?'

'In the house.'

I frowned and shook my head.

'What does he mean?' I asked Natasha in Romanian.

She had a hurried conversation with Simon and Lucy.

'Tomas and Maria had brought many girls from Romania to work for them in London.'

'Serena?'

'They're questioning them all now.'

'Serena was working as a receptionist,' I said.

Lucy and Natasha exchanged a funny look as Natasha translated this.

'I don't think so, Katya.'

'But Maria told me. She said Serena was very happy.'

'No one was happy, Katya. Maria lied to you.'

'Oh.'

I was trying to take this in. I was lied to, and I was unhappy. Had Serena and the other girls been working for people like Mr and Mrs Belanov also? I asked Natasha.

She patted my arm. 'Worse than that, Katya.'

What could be worse than that?

At that moment the door burst open and a tall, grey-haired man and a middle-aged, smartly dressed woman rushed into the room followed by a pretty, blond-haired girl.

'O Simon,' the woman said as she ran to Simon and hugged him tears pouring down both their faces.

'Careful, Mum,' Simon said, wincing. 'That hurts.'

'What have they done to you?'

'Are you OK, son?' the man asked.

There was a flurry of English far too fast for me to understand, but it needed no words for me to see Simon's parents and sister fussing over him and checking to make sure he was alright. I looked down so no one would see how jealous I felt.

'Mum. Dad. Francesca. This is Katya,' Simon said.

'Hello, my dear.'

Simon's mother came over and hugged me.

'Are you alright?'

I nodded. She said something that I didn't understand, but Natasha translated.

'She says what a terrible ordeal.'

'But everything will be all right now?' I asked.

'Hopefully.'

I suddenly felt exhausted. I couldn't stop yawning.

'The doctor will see you and Simon soon and then all the girls,' Natasha said.

'Are they here? Can I see Serena?'

'Soon.'

I could hardly hold myself upright. I just wanted to sleep.

'Come, Katya. We're taking you to a cell. Don't look so alarmed.' Natasha laughed. 'Cells have beds in them. You can have a nap. They won't lock you in. The doctor will see you later.'

I snuggled under the blanket on the bed in the cell and fell fast asleep. I must have slept for ages, but I woke up to find Lucy looking in on me.

'Awake? Feel better?'

I nodded.

'The doctor will see you soon.'

'Simon?'

'Hospital.'

I smiled. Simon would be fine now. He was back with his parents and sister. The black hole of loneliness opened up inside me again.

A lady with a black bag came into the cell.

'Katya?' she asked.

'Yes.'

'How's your English?'

I shook my head. 'Little only.'

She said something to Lucy who went out and fetched Natasha. I asked her what she had been doing.

'Helping the doctors with the other girls.'

The doctor examined me and my cuts and bruises. I answered all her questions and she kept shaking her head and muttering to Natasha who didn't translate. Finally, she put everything back in her bag.

'You can get dressed,' Natasha said. 'The doctor says you will recover from the bruises in time. It will take much longer to recover from what has happened to you.'

'What does she mean?'

'You have been treated very badly. You will need counselling.'

I looked blank.

'Someone will talk to you. Help you understand.'

'Understand what?'

'Maria. Tomas. Mr and Mrs Belanov lied to you. They beat you and imprisoned you. That's wrong.'

'Is it? Maria said it was my choice.'

Natasha shook her head. 'No. They used you. And the other girls.'

'Can I see Serena?'

'Yes. Then they will take you somewhere safe.'

'The children's home?'

'No. To a house where a couple will look after you.'

Natasha took me to another room where Serena and some of the other girls were sitting. They all looked so scared and – well - awful. Their faces were white with traces of make-up still evident. They too had dark rings under their eyes that were red from crying. Some of them were trembling and most sat hunched up wrapped in a blanket. Serena looked ill.

'Katya!' Serena burst into tears. 'I didn't know you were here.'

I ran and hugged her. 'You look awful.'

'Have you seen yourself?' she asked with a tiny smile.

'No.'

'You're all bruised and grubby. What have you been doing?'

'I worked for Mr and Mrs Belanov. I had to clean their house. They were wicked. They beat me and kept me in a cupboard.'

'Poor Katya.' Serena squeezed my shoulders. 'Is Mr Belanov that big Russian with black hair and a sour faced wife?'

I gazed at her wide-eyed. 'Yes. Did you meet him?'

'Yes.' She shuddered. 'Horrible man.'

The look on her face said, 'Don't ask any more'.

'What will happen to us do you think?' I asked.

'I don't know.'

'I am going to some people. I hope they are nice. Natasha said someone would talk to me. I needed it because I don't understand.'

'Dear Katya. Life hasn't been very good for us.'

I shook my head.

She smiled. 'But it will get better.'

Chapter 23

I woke next morning in a warm, comfortable bed.

Late the night before I had been driven to Ben and Madeleine's house. When I arrived, they opened the front door with such kind smiles on their faces, the sort of smiles that made me feel welcome. Madeleine was petite, a little plump with short dark hair, brown eyes blinking behind glasses. Ben was only a little taller with ginger hair and a neat ginger moustache and beard, which had just a little grey sprinkled through it.

They could see how tired I was, so straight away they showed me to a bedroom. I fell asleep quickly, but I kept waking up. Sometimes because my bed was almost too comfortable, but mostly with nightmares.

I kept dreaming that Maria was coming to catch me, or Mr Belanov was strangling Simon and I couldn't help him. I would cry out, but every time Madeleine would come in and hold me close in her arms till my terror passed. She was so warm and comforting.

Over breakfast, I met Ben and Madeleine's son and daughter, Josh and Stephanie, who were both older than me. They were rushing off to school and Ben was going to work. There was a lot of chatter that I did not understand as they grabbed food from the fridge and books and sports kit.

Then, with a quick kiss on their mother's cheek, they were all gone.

I just sat and stared. Was this family life?

Madeleine stayed at home. I helped her clear away the breakfast things.

'No need,' she said.

'Want to.'

She smiled and indicated the dirty plates into a dishwasher. I had never used one before. I was always the dishwasher. I shrugged and she laughed and then showed me how to stack the dishes.

Later, two policemen came with another lady who spoke Romanian. It took a long time to go through my statement about everything that had happened to me from leaving Romania to London to the Belanov's house and Simon's rescue. At the end I was exhausted.

'Sleep?' Madeleine asked after I had eaten lunch.

I nodded and went and lay down on my bed and slept all afternoon. I woke to the sound of people coming through the front door.

I crept downstairs, reluctant to interrupt the family, but Madeleine, hearing my footsteps, took me into the sitting room where Stephanie was watching television. She patted the sofa next to her and I went and sat down. I perched on the edge of the seat, feeling awkward, but Madeleine handed me a cup of tea with a biscuit and a smile.

'Food. Soon.'

'Thank you.'

For the next month, I did very little but eat and sleep. Madeleine took me to the doctors each week to make sure my cuts and bruises were healing. Someone found some Romanian books for me to read, and I loved curling up in a quiet corner and losing myself in the story of someone else's life. Gradually my strength returned, and Madeleine insisted I went out every day for a walk and later to the shops with her.

At first, I was very fearful in case Maria or Mr and Mrs Belanov suddenly appeared and grabbed me. Madeleine kept assuring me they were safely in prison.

'Even if they were free, I don't think they would want to come and find you,' she said.

'Why?'

'You caused them a lot of trouble.' She laughed. 'It was you escaping with Simon's help that led to their arrest.'

'Oh.'

'You have been very brave, Katya.'

Simon phoned quite often at first and so did his mother, but my poor English meant our conversations were very stilted. Gradually, I think we both felt it was important to move on. We had so little to talk about except Simon's rescue of me, and as his wounds healed and he was busy back at school, we chatted less and less.

Once I started to feel better and the bruises faded and the cuts healed, I began to meet with a very kind lady. She talked to me about my life in the orphanage and how Maria had been able to use me and the other girls. Sometimes, we had a group meeting. It was lovely to see everyone else and talk about our experiences though the other girls were very cautious about saying exactly what had happened. They would just exchange fearful glances and shudder.

On one occasion, we were told, 'It is important that you have a dream. Something to aim for. Something you would like to do with your life.'

I was surprised. It had never occurred to me I might decide anything for my life. I had always believed I just had to do as I was told. Someone else would decide what was best for me.

Serena immediately spoke up. 'I shall be a beautician. I have always loved making myself and others beautiful.'

'I want to be a model,' Suzie said, walking up and down, twirling like a model on a catwalk.

The others all had plans.

'Could I be a doctor?' Nadine asked.

'If you work hard,' the lady leading the session said. 'It's important that you have a goal. Something you want to achieve.'

I sat there quietly.

'What about you, Katya?' Serena asked.

'I want to look after children,' I said.

'What? Like the ladies in the home?' Suzie's voice was full of scorn.

'What is wrong with that? Someone has to care for them.'

Everyone looked at me. Serena laughed.

'Go, Katya.'

'Actually, I was thinking of being a nanny or a nursery teacher.'

'That sounds like an excellent idea,' the lady said. 'Here, or in Romania?'

I considered her question. 'Back in Romania I think. It's home.'

Chapter 24

A year later, I sat staring out of the window at the snow-covered peaks of the Romanian mountains. Already the days were becoming shorter and the nights colder. I was both dreading and looking forward to the winter. I loved the snow and sitting round the fire in the evenings, but the winter would be very cold and long.

I was living on a farm with Andrei and Bianca, on the outskirts of a town far away from where I used to live. They were my foster parents and they had three small children. Andrei was a short man but wiry and strong. His arms were muscular from all the physical work he did. His hair was thinning, but I loved the way his grey eyes softened whenever he looked at Bianca. She too was strong, and she picked up her children as if they weighed nothing at all. Her hair was curly, beginning to go grey and she was always tucking it away behind her ears.

My new life was marvellous. Everyone was so kind and for the first time, I felt loved. I went to school, and I was making friends. I discovered I was not as stupid as everyone thought. If I worked hard, I could do well. I had even started going to a gym club. In the afternoons, I looked after Andrei and Bianca's children or helped with the chores. I had not let go of my dream of becoming a nanny or work in a nursery.

With good food and exercise, I had grown taller, and I no longer looked like a girl. I was a young woman. All the counselling in England and Ben and Madeleine's kindness meant I had grown in confidence. I was no longer little Katya.

Sometime after I arrived back in Romania, I heard from Serena that Maria and the Belanovs had committed many crimes and would not be spending many years in prison. They even caught Tomas as he tried to cross the English Channel and he too was in prison. His car was full of the evidence of his crimes. I knew they would never come looking for me no, so I felt safe, and I could sleep at night without awful nightmares.

Serena had stayed in England and was learning to be a beautician, just as she always wanted. I was happy for her though I missed her and wished I could meet her again. Life was never dull when Serena was around, though I think her awful experiences, which she never talked about to me, had turned her from a happy-go-lucky girl, full of mischief into a more serious young lady. But I knew it would take a lot to put out that fun-loving sparkle in her eyes.

I enjoyed the company of the girls my age at school. We laughed and chatted together. Shy Katya who never knew what was going on had transformed from an ugly duckling into the beginnings of a graceful swan.

Some of the girls though worried me. They were often on their phones to a man who met them outside school and had been making all sorts of promises and buying them gifts. When they started talking about a new life in Germany or England, it made my blood run cold.

'Have nothing to do with him is my advice. I went to England expecting a new life and I had a terrible time.'

'Really! Tell us,' they said.

So I told them about Maria and my life as a slave with Mr. and Mrs. Belanov.

'You're making it up,' they said.

'I can assure you. I am not.'

They stared at me.

'Believe me or not. It's what happened.'

I turned away and left them. I hoped they would make better choices than I had.

My life was good. I now had the life I always wanted. I had a family. I had friends and I had a future.

Also by Christine Ottaway

Nick North series

Adventure stories for middle grade readers aged 10 – 12

Nick North: Blood Quest

An out-of-world experience on Bonfire turns Nick North from schoolboy to dragon slayer to hero of the hour as he rights wrongs from the past and discovers his true identity.

Great book. I loved the easy move from the everyday to the fantastic.

Nick North: War Zone

From the battlefields of the First World War to a field hospital and into the present-day Nick faces terrible dangers to free Leone's family from their past.

Some great descriptions in the book of life in the trenches as well as relating the past to the present.

A terrific read for adults as well as teens, I thoroughly enjoyed it and wish there were more books like this for my grandsons.

Nick North: Cross Wires

The third book in the series. Nick and Ashley find themselves in Nazi Germany in the Second World War where tragic events and heroism start a trail of animosity entangling Nick and his adversary, Alex Jenkins, but can they unravel terrible injustices to free themselves from the past?

Nick North: Into Africa

Nick has a terrible dream of a slave being beaten to death, hundreds of years ago. Two weeks later, whilst on holiday in Cape Town, South Africa, he visits a wine estate, the place where he saw the slave being murdered. The Shepherd calls him to right this terrible wrong and to cleanse the land of his bloodshed. Nick becomes immersed in an exciting adventure to unravel the tragic injustice of generations of one slave family.